"And tell me again why you seem to be on their side after they tried to steal your horse?" asked the redhead.

"I'm not," Clint said. "Now why don't you tell me why you and your men decided to drag me off the street when I signed on to help you."

The redhead leaned in close. "We don't want the help of some chickenshit tenderfoot with a loud mouth."

"You've got one second to take that back," Clint warned.

"Or what?" the redhead scoffed. "You'll—"

Clint drove his knee into the redhead's stomach with enough force to double him over. But the redhead was a tough fellow and straightened up. However, he was knocked aside by the second deputy. Then Clint twisted his entire body around so his hip was against Frank's midsection. Once he had a good pivot point, Clint swung Frank into the redhead.

Allowing the men to catch their breath, Clint told them, "You had that coming for flapping your gums. Since we're working together, we can call it even."

Upon a quick nod from the redhead, Frank snapped a fist at Clint. Clint sent a jab, hitting Frank in the mouth.

When Clint faced the redhead again, he saw the deputy reach for the gun holstered at his side. In a flicker of motion, Clint drew his modified Colt and aimed it at the deputy.

"Last chance to call it even," Clint said. "What do you say?"

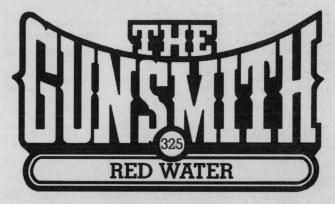

THE GUNSMITH

325

RED WATER

J. R. ROBERTS

JOVE BOOKS, NEW YORK

THE BERKLEY PUBLISHING GROUP
Published by the Penguin Group
Penguin Group (USA) Inc.
375 Hudson Street, New York, New York 10014, USA
Penguin Group (Canada), 90 Eglinton Avenue East, Suite 700, Toronto, Ontario M4P 2Y3, Canada
(a division of Pearson Penguin Canada Inc.)
Penguin Books Ltd., 80 Strand, London WC2R 0RL, England
Penguin Group Ireland, 25 St. Stephen's Green, Dublin 2, Ireland (a division of Penguin Books Ltd.)
Penguin Group (Australia), 250 Camberwell Road, Camberwell, Victoria 3124, Australia
(a division of Pearson Australia Group Pty. Ltd.)
Penguin Books India Pvt. Ltd., 11 Community Centre, Panchsheel Park, New Delhi—110 017, India
Penguin Group (NZ), 67 Apollo Drive, Rosedale, North Shore 0632, New Zealand
(a division of Pearson New Zealand Ltd.)
Penguin Books (South Africa) (Pty.) Ltd., 24 Sturdee Avenue, Rosebank, Johannesburg 2196,
South Africa

Penguin Books Ltd., Registered Offices: 80 Strand, London WC2R 0RL, England

This is a work of fiction. Names, characters, places, and incidents either are the product of the author's imagination or are used fictitiously, and any resemblance to actual persons, living or dead, business establishments, events, or locales is entirely coincidental.

RED WATER

A Jove Book / published by arrangement with the author

PRINTING HISTORY
Jove edition / January 2009

Copyright © 2009 by Robert J. Randisi.
Cover illustration by Sergio Giovine.

ISBN: 978-0-515-14574-8

JOVE®
Jove Books are published by The Berkley Publishing Group,
a division of Penguin Group (USA) Inc.,
375 Hudson Street, New York, New York 10014.
JOVE® is a registered trademark of Penguin Group (USA) Inc.
The "J" design is a trademark of Penguin Group (USA) Inc.

PRINTED IN THE UNITED STATES OF AMERICA

10 9 8 7 6 5 4 3 2 1

ONE

Clint Adams was never the sort of man who took life easily. Some fellows were perfectly content to lie back and let themselves be carried along by whatever current was strong enough to move them. Some men didn't care if they ever moved at all. Others didn't have enough gumption to do anything about it if they weren't pleased with the way things were going.

Although Clint rarely got a chance to kick his feet up and let out a few relaxed breaths, the truth was he simply couldn't sit still for very long. Most times, he felt an itch that carried him from one spot to another, poking his nose in where it didn't belong and seeing things through when most men would have gladly turned their back on them.

There were always deeds to be done, but not when a man was too content to sit on his backside. Every so often, however, Clint was more than happy to indulge.

Plenty of deeds came to mind when Clint thought of indulgence. Most such things could be thought of as wreaking havoc on a man's body or even smudging his soul. For a man like Clint Adams, indulgences were a little simpler.

Clint was savoring one such indulgence as he sat with

his back against a perfectly sloped rock. His legs were stretched out in front of him and his hat was situated so it covered the upper portion of his face. One arm rested across his belly and he lifted the other to place a cigar between his lips.

The tobacco was fresh and expensive. What made the cigar even sweeter was the fact that it had been free. Clint had had a fairly good stretch at the card tables in Wichita, and his winnings had nearly doubled thanks to a drunken knife-throwing contest. Having been the only man to stick his blade anywhere close to the mark on the saloon's wall was enough to win him several dollars, plenty of drinks, and a few very expensive cigars. Actually, considering the state of the other men tossing those knives, Clint could have won the contest by being the only man to keep from drawing anyone's blood on a bad throw.

He left Wichita with a smile on his face and hadn't had a need to draw his pistol once. For a man widely known as the Gunsmith, that was no easy feat.

Clint had ridden northwest with his sights set on Wyoming for no other reason than a whim to get a look at some mountains. There was enough money in his pockets to keep him going for a while and there was no reason for him to be anywhere else. All in all, it wasn't a bad spot to be. While Clint normally wasn't much of a vagrant, drifting had its charms. As he drew in a puff of his cigar, he smiled and stretched out a bit more.

Closing his eyes, Clint could hear Eclipse's hooves scraping against the ground. The Darley Arabian stallion grazed in a patch of grass a few yards away. Much like his owner, Eclipse had been restless at first but quickly adjusted to the slower pace of the last few days. The black horse didn't even need to wear his saddle or bridle. He moseyed from one spot to another and wasn't in much of a hurry to do anything else.

Clint lifted his chin and expelled a smoky breath. The fragrant smoke curled through the air and was carried away by a slow breeze that was cool enough to announce the approaching dusk. Even after the smoke was out of him, Clint pushed the rest of the air from his lungs just because it felt good to do so.

Sometimes, a man just needed to enjoy the simple things.

As Clint's breath faded away, his ears caught nothing but the sound of rustling grass and Eclipse's contented sniffing. Savoring the moment, Clint relished the absolute silence that followed.

The silence lasted for all of three seconds.

If Clint hadn't been so relaxed, he could have very easily overlooked the sound completely. Voices were drifting through the air. Clint pulled his hat down a bit lower and tried to ignore them. When Clint heard the voices struggle to hush each other as they drew closer, he knew someone was trying to creep up on him.

Clint batted around the idea of pretending to be asleep, but that could prove to be especially dangerous if the men sneaking up on him meant to do any harm. He also considered silencing the approaching men with a few well-placed shots from his Colt, but that would only have created more noise.

Reluctantly, Clint pulled himself to his feet so he could circle around to get the drop on whoever had ruined such a peaceful day.

TWO

Three men led their horses to the spot where Clint had set up his camp. All they found when they got there was an empty patch of grass, a few trees, and a short pile of burnt wood.

The man at the front of the trio had a round face covered in rough stubble. Although he appeared to be somewhere in his early twenties, his squinty eyes looked to have seen more than his share of trouble in that time. The more the man's eyes darted back and forth, the narrower and more suspicious they became. "Where the hell is he?"

"How should I know?" asked the man at the back of the trio. He was the first man's senior by at least ten years, but wore his age well. Short, dark hair and a thin beard framed a narrow face. He walked with a swagger even though the only one watching him was his horse. "You were the one who spotted him."

"I did spot him, Chris," the younger man replied.

Mimicking the tone of that response, Chris said, "I know you did, *Harvey*. Now it would be useful if you could spot him again."

The man in between the other two was only slightly

taller than his companions, but carried himself as if he could tower over both of them even if they were in their saddles. A muscular black man somewhere in his early thirties, he dressed in simple buckskins beneath a tattered formal coat. He smiled, but didn't make a sound.

Twisting around as if he could hear the black man's expression change, Harvey snapped, "What's so goddamn funny?"

Although his smile dimmed somewhat, the black man did not avert his eyes. In fact, he focused them on the younger man intensely enough to cause Harvey to look away first.

"Go on and push Samuel some more, Harvey," Chris chided. "I always like to see a good fight, though I don't know how good it would be."

Since Samuel wasn't adding any fuel to the younger man's fire, Harvey shifted his gaze toward Chris. "I don't like it when you call me that. Jus' call me what everyone else does."

Chris glared at the younger man as if he were struggling to keep himself from taking a swing at him. After gnawing on the inside of his cheek for a moment, he grunted. "Fine. Now can you spot this asshole again or not?"

"If I could, don't you think I would have?"

"You sure you even saw anyone or did you just see smoke from that cooking fire?"

"There was someone here!" Whipping his head back around so he was once again facing forward, the younger man furrowed his brow and muttered, "Least I thought there was."

Before Chris could get out the insult he'd prepared, something heavy thumped against the ground no more than five yards to the men's left. All three of them turned toward the sound as their hands went for the guns at their hips. Only the youngest of them cleared leather.

"You hear that?" Harvey snapped. "I told you I—"

"Shut up," Chris snarled. He glanced over at Samuel and pointed away from the sound before moving his finger in a quick half-circle. Nodding, the black man moved away from the group to get behind whatever had made that sound.

"He's got it covered," Chris said. "I'll swing around the other way."

"What do you want me to do?" Harvey asked.

"Keep walking straight. If that fella you spotted is around here, we'll flush him out. When we do . . ."

"I know what to do," the younger man groused.

Chris nodded the way he might show his approval to a bright-eyed puppy. "Just don't shoot too soon and try not to hit any one of us."

Harvey's lips moved without letting any sound escape them. Judging by the look on his face, the words he'd choked back were anything but friendly.

As Harvey inched his way forward, Chris drew his .45 and held it at hip level. Every step Chris took, he picked up some speed and hunkered down a little more until he was practically scurrying through the weeds on all fours. Harvey took a quick look in the other direction and was barely able to catch sight of Samuel. For a man his size, Samuel never had any trouble turning into a ghost when he needed to.

After taking a few more steps, Harvey's ears pricked up at the sound of more movement in front of him. He bent at the knees, but knew it was useless to try to hide since he couldn't move the way Samuel could. Plastering a defiant snarl on his face, he tightened his grip upon the weathered Cavalry-model pistol that had been glued to his side since he'd left home. There were better models out there, but the young man had learned to make this one sing. Just feeling it in his grasp was enough to put some more steam into his stride.

The small clearing was only a few paces away, so Harvey covered the distance quickly. When he got to the smoldering pile of firewood, he kicked it over as if the charred sticks had done him wrong. Lifting his chin a bit, he pulled in a breath that was still flavored by the scent of expensive tobacco. Just as he was feeling confident in his tracking abilities, Harvey jumped at a voice that cracked through the air like a gunshot.

"State your business!" Clint's voice came from a direction that none of the three other men had anticipated.

Harvey spun around quick enough to feel a little dizzy when he came to a stop. His two partners weren't so fast to turn, but they did stop in their tracks to find who'd just spoken.

"Who's there?" Harvey asked. "Show yerself!"

After a few seconds, Chris circled around the camp. When Harvey looked over at him, the older man pointed in the direction of Clint's voice and then started moving that way. Samuel wasn't in sight, but Harvey knew he had to be close by.

"What's the matter?" Harvey challenged. "You scared to stand up so we can see ya? All we want is to say howdy."

Just when it seemed that there was no reply forthcoming, Clint answered, "Men don't say howdy with their guns drawn."

Hearing Clint's voice come from a new direction entirely caused all three of the other men to stop and look about as though they were being pestered by a swarm of invisible moths. When Harvey finally did allow his eyes to settle on one spot, it seemed more because he was tired than because he'd actually found what he'd been searching for.

The longer he waited, the more aggravated Chris became. The sour expression on his face only turned uglier when he heard Clint's voice again.

"You men here to rob me?" Clint asked.

Snapping his head toward a new direction altogether, Chris hollered, "You're the one sneaking around, damn it! Stand up so's we can see you!"

"You are here to rob me."

Behind Chris and to his left, Samuel let out a short whistle. Chris turned to find the dark-skinned man crouching in the grass and pointing toward something that brought a smirk to Chris's face.

"I see your horse, mister," Chris announced. "We'll just help ourselves to the animal since you're of a mind to run and hide instead of share some coffee with a few thirsty cowboys." When he didn't get a response, Chris turned to Harvey and said, "Go fetch that horse."

"You don't order me around," Harvey growled. His hackles stayed up for a few heartbeats before he shrugged and said, "I'll go get the horse, since that's why we was here in the first place."

THREE

As soon as Clint heard the youngest of the three men mention stealing Eclipse, he didn't mind being disturbed in the midst of his relaxing day. On the contrary, watching the trio scatter and sneak around while he threw rocks at them and made noises to draw them off was more than enough entertainment to keep Clint occupied.

Eclipse had thrown things off a bit by wandering a little too far in the wrong direction, but that wasn't anything Clint couldn't handle. All he needed to do was wait for the men to get close enough to the Darley Arabian before he made a move of his own. Crawling on his belly through one of the many patches of tall weeds surrounding his camp, Clint stuck his head up just enough to get a look at what the men were doing.

The kid was making a line straight for Eclipse while the older one circled to the right. Clint had a harder time keeping track of Samuel, but he figured that the black man was somewhere off to the left. Holding his hat against one cheek to throw his voice in another direction, Clint shouted, "Leave now before someone gets hurt."

Harvey spun on the balls of his feet toward the sound

of Clint's voice. Then he shifted toward the direction of Clint's words drifting in, thanks to the wind and a well-placed hat brim. "Only one to be hurt will be you if'n you try to step up. You'd be wise to scat if you knew what was good for you!"

Clint could hear the nervousness in Harvey's voice. It made him sound even more like a kid than anyone who had any business with a gun in his hand. But the guns were still out, so Clint wasn't about to take any chances. He pressed his belly against the ground and crawled toward Chris. Once he was in a good spot not too far from his original camp, Clint stretched his neck up to get a look at the others.

When he heard the rustle of movement behind him, it was too late for Clint to do anything about it. When he felt the touch of sharpened steel against his throat, Clint knew it was time to make the move he'd been planning.

Clint's arms snapped up and out in a blur of motion. If Samuel meant to say anything before cutting Clint's throat, he didn't get the chance since his knife was forced back from its target. Having locked one hand around Samuel's wrist to push the blade away from his throat, Clint sent his other elbow straight back and into the man's gut.

The moment he felt the impact of his elbow against tensed muscle, Clint pulled it back and delivered another blow hot on the heels of the first. That made it a lot easier for him to twist around and pull Samuel's knife hand along for the ride. With a bit of torque in the proper spot and some muscle applied at the proper time, Clint was able to lift Samuel off his feet, heft him over one shoulder, and drop him onto the ground.

Samuel landed with a pained grunt and immediately scrambled to his feet. Before he could get there, one of Clint's boots knocked into him with just enough force to send him rolling onto his side. Samuel's second landing was much more awkward than the first, so recovering from it wasn't nearly as easy.

Now that he'd put Samuel down, Clint ended up with the man's knife in his possession. He threw the blade into the grass and looked around for the other two would-be horse thieves. Just as he'd suspected, Harvey and Chris were coming straight at him. Before either of them could get a shot off, Clint let out a sharp whistle.

Behind Harvey and Chris, Eclipse snapped his head around to look at Clint as his hooves began churning up some dirt. The stallion reacted to the signal out of sheer reflex and knew Clint needed him right away. Eclipse wasn't about to slow down until he got to Clint's side and he sure as hell wasn't about to politely ask either of the two men in front of him to clear a path.

"Jesus!" Chris yelped as he dove to one side before Eclipse could trample him.

Harvey fired a quick shot that hissed well above Clint's head. After that, he was more than happy to follow his partner's lead.

Even if Clint could have delivered orders to the stallion, he couldn't have asked for a better showing from Eclipse. Even though the Darley Arabian was careful to jump over the two men, his massive frame hurdled Harvey and Chris with just enough clearance to force both of them to hug the ground and pray to live through the experience. In a matter of seconds, Eclipse was within Clint's reach.

Clint reached out to grab on to the saddle horn so he could pull himself onto Eclipse's back. The moment he was settled, Clint snapped the reins to get Eclipse moving again.

"Shoot him!" Chris hollered.

Before either of the would-be horse thieves could reply to that, Clint gave a response of his own. He drew his modified

Colt and fired a pair of shots into the ground within a few feet of both men. Now that he was higher off the ground, Clint was also able to pick out where Samuel had gone to.

The muscular man in the formal coat had gotten to within a few yards of Clint. Now that he'd been spotted, he dropped to one knee and lifted his gun.

Clint shifted his aim and was forced to make a quick decision. In the blink of an eye, he had to decide whether or not to kill the man at the other end of his Colt's barrel. Samuel had his gun drawn and he surely intended to shoot, but the fight was almost over anyhow. In the end, Samuel's life was saved by the fact that Clint was still feeling the effects of the last few relaxing days. Rather than put a bullet through Samuel's heart, Clint adjusted his aim and fired.

The modified Colt barked once more and sent a piece of hot lead whizzing past Samuel's temple. The near-miss brought an angry scowl of astonishment and fear to his face.

Clint tapped his heels against Eclipse's sides, which got the stallion charging once more. Leaning forward, Clint fired his last few rounds toward Harvey and Chris. Those shots were too quick to be very accurate, but they served their purpose well enough when they caused both targets to dive for cover before returning fire.

In a matter of seconds, Eclipse had run past the two men and headed for another set of targets. These targets were the horses the trio had ridden to Clint's camp. Although Clint wasn't about to become a horse thief himself, he wasn't about to make it easy for the trio to follow him.

Waving his empty pistol over his head, Clint hooted and hollered like a crazy man as he thundered toward the horses. The animals weren't spooked by gunfire, but they sure as hell were rattled at what was thundering toward them now. The three horses cleared a path for Eclipse to charge by on his first pass.

On Eclipse's second pass, the three horses got moving even faster.

After Eclipse took a third run at them, the horses bolted in different directions.

Satisfied that the horses wouldn't get back to their riders anytime soon, Clint pointed Eclipse's nose to the west and snapped the reins. The horse thieves fired shots at his back, but their aim was off and Clint was quickly out of their range.

Clint spent the next several miles of his ride letting Eclipse run to his heart's content and doubling back every now and then to make sure he wasn't being followed. Not only had he shaken the three thieves, but Clint had broken camp with a smile on his face.

"Now that," Clint chuckled to himself, "was fun."

FOUR

When Clint arrived at the town of Red Water, he was greeted by everything short of a parade. Banners were hung from nearly every post and brightly colored streamers flowed from most of the windows. There was even a band playing loudly to the cheers of an appreciative crowd. Of course, that band consisted of two banjos and a harmonica, but the crowd was cheering all the same.

Clint rode down Sales Street, taking in the sights and shaking his head at it all. A confused smile had taken residence upon his face and wasn't about to drift away so long as the hectic music continued to fill the air around him. His gaze was captured by a woman in her late thirties wearing a pale blue dress and matching ribbons in her chestnut-colored hair.

"You here for Founder's Day?" she asked.

"Founder's Day?" Clint replied. "You mean this commotion isn't to welcome me into town?"

The woman laughed and playfully smacked Clint's leg. "No, silly," she told him with just a hint of a drunken slur in her voice. "It's Founder's Day. If you like, I can welcome you into town, though."

"I think I would like that."

"Well, then," she said as she dipped into a quick curtsey, "welcome to town."

"Thanks for that," Clint replied with a tip of his hat. "I'm Clint Adams. Who might you be?"

Just as the woman was about to answer him, another woman dashed up to her and tugged at her arm. The second woman was a little younger, but also had a little more meat on her bones. The smile on her face, however, was just as infectious as she said, "Come on, Allie! They're judging the cakes!"

"Did I bake a cake for the contest?" Allie asked with a bit more of the slur showing through in her voice.

"Yes, you did, now come on!" With that, the younger woman dragged Allie away.

All Clint could do was watch her go. Not only had the younger woman inadvertently answered his question, but she also showed him where the festivities were being held. He rode along behind the two women, allowing himself to be led to a long row of tables covered with food of all kinds. He swung down from his saddle to tie Eclipse to a post before the stallion got too close to any of the groups of children playing around the noisy band.

The sun was halfway down, which bathed the town in a dull glow befitting its name. Red Water was anything but tired, however, and the party just seemed to grow wilder with every step Clint took. Kegs were set up near the food tables and punch bowls were either being filled or had already been completely overturned.

Clint hopped onto the boardwalk running along a row of storefronts to allow a group of dancing couples to spin past him. Watching them go, it was all Clint could do to keep from laughing. But since nobody else around him was restraining themselves so much, he just gave in and laughed.

"What's so funny?" someone asked from Clint's left.

Hearing that question reminded him of the conversation he'd overheard between the three horse thieves not too long ago. Unlike those thieves, however, this question was asked in a tone that was anything but threatening. The voice doing the talking was a whole lot sweeter, too.

Clint looked over to find the younger woman who'd dragged Allie away. Allie was nowhere to be seen, leaving Clint to get a good look at Allie's friend. She was definitely younger and just a bit heavier than Allie. She wasn't fat, by any means, and looked even better now that Clint had a moment to take in the sight of her. Large, round breasts were wrapped in a dark green dress that hung nicely over a set of equally rounded hips. At the moment, the young woman placed her hands on her hips and fixed Clint with an intense glare.

"You were laughing," she scolded.

"Isn't that allowed?"

"Only if you tell me the joke."

Clint opened his arms to motion to everything around him. "Just taking it all in. Trying to, anyway."

Quickly, she nodded. "That's as good a reason as any. Are you hungry?"

"Starving."

"Then come along," she said as she looped her arm around Clint's and dragged him almost as forcefully as she'd dragged Allie. "There's not a lot left, but there should be enough to fill you up." Suddenly, she stopped. "Wait a second. It's not a good idea to socialize with strange men."

Clint only had to look at the sly grin on her face to know she wasn't seriously thinking twice about anything.

"What's your name?" she asked.

"Clint Adams."

Letting go of his arm so she could hop in front of him,

she held out a hand and waited for him to shake it. "Gwendolyn Price," she told him. After that, she hopped back to her previous spot beside Clint and took hold of his arm again. "Now we're not strangers. Let's get something to eat."

Now that he was closer to her, Clint tacked on a few more years to his original estimate of Gwendolyn's age. Even so, that was only a reflection of a few lines around her eyes and a confidence in her voice that young girls simply didn't have. Gwendolyn was somewhere in her late twenties, but had a spring in her step that would always make her seem younger. That spring was echoed in her curly, dark blond locks of hair, which bounced against her shoulders with every step.

"Since we're not strangers, why don't I call you Gwen?" Clint asked.

"If you want to be that familiar, you might as well dance with me after you eat."

"I've got no problem with that whatsoever."

FIVE

Even after he'd stuffed himself on scraps of ham, cold potato salad, and a sliver of leftover pie, Clint had no idea who'd founded Red Water. Judging by the commotion that went on well past sunset, Clint figured that the founders were very well liked.

A few fireworks crackled overhead as soon as it was dark enough to see them. Once they were spent, some of the rowdier drunks fired some shots into the air before staggering to one of the nearby saloons. That left only the band to make noise in the street, which they did impressively well. Despite the fact that the musicians only seemed to know four songs, they didn't show any signs of tiring.

The band members weren't the only ones with so much stamina. Once Gwen's feet got moving, Clint couldn't find any way to stop her. Of course, since Gwen's dancing kept her pressed against him as she bounced to the beat of the music, Clint didn't exactly want to stop her. He just hung on and enjoyed the ride.

When he heard the band start into the third of their four songs, Clint launched into the steps he'd been practicing the other dozen or so times it had been played. His feet barely started to gain momentum before Gwen latched on to his arm and pulled him away from the street.

"Do you pull everyone around like that?" Clint asked.

"Only when they need to be somewhere quick," Gwen replied.

"I don't need to be anywhere else at the moment."

Wheeling around to face him as she continued to backpedal in the direction she'd been taking him, Gwen cocked her eyebrow and asked, "Is that so?"

There was only a half-moon out, but it was bright enough to cast her face in a cool, pale glow. Clint didn't hide the fact that his eyes wandered along the front of her body as he said, "Yeah. That's so. Where are you taking me?"

"Over there," she replied as she took his hand and spun back around to see where she was going.

"Is that a corral?"

"Uh huh."

"You're taking me to a corral?"

"No," Gwen told him. "I'm taking you to the lot behind the corral." With that, she turned to face Clint once again and then fell backward onto the lumpy remains of some hay bales.

Unable and unwilling to shake loose of Gwen's grip, Clint allowed himself to be pulled down as well. Even though Gwen cushioned his fall more than the hay, there was enough spread out on the ground beneath her to make them both comfortable. The moment he was off his feet, Clint wrapped an arm around Gwen's waist and pulled her close. He'd been holding on to her throughout all the dancing, but it was a whole lot better with her beneath him.

"God, I've been waiting for this all night." She sighed.

"I would've started in sooner, but the band was watching."

Anxiously working Clint's belt buckle, Gwen pulled it open and then got to work on his jeans. "Well, nobody's watching now apart from a few horses."

"Right about now, I don't even care if the rest of the town's looking over my shoulder," Clint said as he felt Gwen's fingers wrap around his stiffening cock.

Gwen laughed and opened her legs so Clint could settle between them. Shifting her backside within the hay, she made it as easy as possible for him to gather her skirts up and pull her bloomers down. Once that baggy material was out of the way, Clint could feel nothing but the soft, warm skin of her thigh. Moving his hand a bit higher, he quickly found the tuft of curly hair between her legs.

"The rest of the town's got plenty to do." Gwen sighed. "And you've got me to keep you busy."

"I'll drink to that."

Clint only needed to run his fingers up and down a few times along the lips of her pussy to get her nice and wet. When he took his hand away, Gwen grabbed hold of the front of his shirt and pulled him on top of her as her legs wrapped around him. She shifted her hips until she felt Clint's erection rubbing against her and then smiled contentedly as he pushed it inside.

A stray breeze sent a chill down Clint's spine as a few drunks got into a fight no more than fifty yards away. Being out in the open, Clint could hear almost every sound in town but he didn't pay any mind to it. All he cared about were the little noises Gwen made as he thrust in and out of her. His hands rustled through the hay when he reached around to grab the inviting curve of her backside. Once he had a good grip, Clint pulled her to him and buried his rigid cock in her.

Gwen arched her back and moaned. Her arms tightened around him and her fingernails dug all the way through

Clint's shirt. When he began sliding in and out again, she matched his rhythm with her own movements until their bodies dug a deep trench in the tussled straw.

Clint felt his knees start to slip as the hay shifted beneath him. He managed to keep from tumbling over, but still wound up on his side next to Gwen. Rather than wait for him to get situated again, she shifted onto her side so her plump buttocks were against Clint's stomach. After draping one leg up and over him, she reached down to guide him back to the wet lips of her pussy.

Clint entered her from behind while both of them lay on their sides. It would have been difficult to do on a proper mattress, but the hay conformed to them no matter how they angled their bodies. Since Clint was already inside of her, he started pumping again. He could tell that he was hitting a good spot inside of Gwen because she tensed against him and reached back to grab at his arm.

"Holy . . ." She gasped. "Oh . . . oh my God."

While he hadn't been sure about the position in which they'd wound up, Clint knew it was a winner the moment Gwen's pussy tightened around him and she shook with a powerful orgasm. He slowed his pace a bit before she cried out loud enough to be heard by the whole town. Just when she was regaining control of herself, Clint drove into her again.

The move caught her by surprise, but Gwen was too worn out to make much noise. She grabbed a few handfuls of straw and wriggled her backside against him. Now it was her turn to hang on for the ride.

Clint grabbed her hips in both hands. That way, he could move her back and forth as he slid in and out of her. As his climax rushed toward him, Clint pounded into her harder and harder. Fortunately, Gwen's body was built for just such an occasion and she was well into her second orgasm by the time Clint was overtaken by his own. With one more strong thrust, he exploded inside of her. After that, he could only lie back and try to catch his breath.

Gwen moved around so she was lying with her face against Clint's chest. The cool air brushed over her skin, which was made to look even creamier thanks to the pale moonlight.

Grinning, Clint said, "Happy Founder's Day."

SIX

As comfortable as that pile of straw behind the corral had become, Clint didn't spend the entire night there. While he and Gwen had been pulling themselves together, they were nearly discovered by some folks looking for their horses. Clint felt like a kid escaping with a pocketful of stolen candy sticks when he led Gwen away from there in a rush. It also made it easier for them to part ways.

"Go on and get before someone thinks you stole something," Clint told her.

Gwen blinked excitedly and asked, "You want to come with me?"

"I saw a hotel on Sales Street. I'll go there, so nobody gets the wrong idea about us."

"Too late for that." She chuckled.

When the folks looking for their horses walked into sight, Clint gave Gwen a quick tap on the rump. That, combined with the exhilaration already running through her, was enough to get Gwen moving. Clint had to laugh as he watched her scamper away. When he noticed the folks near the corral looking at him with no small amount of confusion on their faces, he tipped his hat to them and strolled toward Sales Street.

The hotel Clint had spotted was the Well Water Inn at the far end of Sales Street. Even though the festivities hadn't quite dried up just yet, the inn was far enough away so the noise was at a tolerable level. The band had packed it in for the night, and that made things a lot easier to bear. Clint rented the last available room, set his things in a corner, and then dropped onto the bed.

After all he'd done that day, Clint fell asleep on top of the covers with his clothes and boots still on. Sometime during the night, he crawled under the sheets, but he didn't quite recall when that had happened. When he awoke the next morning, it was to the scent of fried eggs and bacon.

"Well, well," he mused as he sat up and rubbed his eyes. "Seems like my luck is still holding up."

Breakfast was a quiet affair. Judging by the pall in the dining room, Clint figured that someone had died or that the folks having their meals were still feeling the bite from all the liquor they'd consumed the night before. Just to test the waters, Clint scooted his chair out a bit rougher than he could have.

"Aw, hell," one of the nearby diners groaned.

Since that fellow and everyone else in the room winced as if the noise were a bullet ripping through their heads, Clint guessed that the liquor was the cause of the somber mood around him. If there was any doubt of that, it was cleared up when the inn's owner practically skipped into the dining room with a kettle in one hand and a plate of bacon in the other.

"Anyone want more coffee?" she asked.

"Quiet, Donna!" another of the guests snarled.

Ignoring the sour words, Donna looked around hopefully. Seeing that Clint was the only one not glaring daggers at her, she extended her other arm. "What about you? More bacon?"

"Sounds perfect," Clint replied.

Donna smiled widely and walked over to Clint's table. Lowering her voice to a whisper, she said, "I see you know how to control yourself during a Founder's Day celebration."

"More or less."

"That's good to see!"

Several more guests waved at her or groaned into their plates, which only brought a critical scowl to Donna's oval face. Straight brown hair was tied into two braids and hung down along the front of her shoulders. Clint guessed it was no fluke that her hair and the ribbon tied at the end of her braids were a perfect match to her brown and red dress.

"Will you be staying for the festivities tonight, Mr. Adams?" Donna asked.

"Will they be anything like last night?"

"Even better! There's a cakewalk down at the church, a picnic starting at one o'clock, and more dancing." Sensing the expectant eyes that were fixed upon her from every other seat in the dining room, she added, "And more tables set up by the saloons, of course."

That last part was well received by the others, no matter how much they were hurting at the moment.

Donna rolled her eyes, but put on a friendly face for Clint as she said, "I'm entering two cakes, myself. They're my specialty."

Lifting his coffee cup after helping himself to a few perfectly cooked strips of bacon, Clint replied, "Wild horses couldn't drag me away."

Just when Clint thought Donna's smile couldn't be any brighter, he was proven wrong. "Wonderful." She beamed. "That's just wonderful." With that, she turned and started to make her way back to the kitchen.

Clint had just set down his cup when Donna stopped and spun back around to face the room. "Oh, and the marshal is in town."

"Probably lookin' for those saloon tables," one of the aching guests suggested.

"No," Donna scolded. "Well . . . maybe. He asked me to ask my guests to stop by Tanner Hall whenever they got a chance."

"What for?"

Since one guest in particular had been needling Donna the most, she fixed him with a particularly nasty scowl. "There's been some problems with robbers and such that might cut Founder's Day short."

That statement couldn't have gotten a worse reaction if it had been followed by a rabid dog being let loose in the room.

"What?" the crankiest diner asked.

Obviously proud of what she'd stirred up, Donna said, "That's right. He wants to speak to you men, so go pay him a visit." With that, she used her hip to bump open the door behind her and walked into the kitchen.

Clint had to chuckle at the way Donna handled her guests. Since one of the things she'd said struck a chord with him, Clint decided he, too, would see what was on the lawman's mind.

SEVEN

Tanner Hall was a real fancy name for a not-so-fancy place. Despite the ornate sign nailed to the front of the single-floor building, the hall wasn't much more than a billiard room. Clint stepped inside the place to find a few small square tables scattered between three billiard tables covered in faded red felt. There was a short bar at the far end of the room that was tended by a tall man wearing a checked shirt.

Spotting Clint, the bartender took an empty glass from under the bar and asked, "What can I get for you, mister?"

"I'm just here to see the marshal," Clint replied.

"What about a drink?"

Blinking once, Clint stepped a little closer to the bar. "Nothing to drink. I just heard the marshal wanted to—"

"You need to order a drink. That's the rule here at Tanner Hall."

"But I don't want anything to drink."

"Then you can't stay."

Before the anger in Clint's gut could flare up too much, he noticed a man wearing a black suit waving at him from one of the small square tables. The next thing Clint noticed was the badge pinned to the man's lapel.

"There's the marshal," Clint said. "I'll just go over there and see what he wants."

When the bartender reached across the bar, he almost lost his hand. Clint snapped his arm away so quickly that he knocked the bartender's knuckles against the polished wooden surface.

"There's a sign posted, asshole," the bartender growled. "One drink minimum."

"Fine, send it over to the marshal's table."

"What'll you have?" the barkeep asked.

"Surprise me."

The bartender rubbed his bruised hand and then straightened his shirt. "There, now. Was that so hard?"

Clint choked back the urge to slam his fist into the man's smug face, then walked over to the marshal. "I was told you wanted to speak to folks staying at the Well Water Inn?"

The lawman was a squat fellow with a trimmed mustache that spread along the entire top of his upper lip and was cut short at either end of his mouth. A dented hat sat on the table, next to a tall glass filled with water. His head looked like an overly ripe squash with a broken ring of hair connecting the back of one ear to the back of the other. Judging by the long strands that sprouted irregularly from the top of his scalp, he hadn't quite come to terms with the fact that he would soon be completely bald.

After taking a few seconds to size Clint up, the lawman gave him one upward nod. "Yeah. I wanted everyone to come talk to me. Have a seat."

Clint pulled up a chair and sat down. "I suppose you were forced to buy that water?"

"Huh?"

"Never mind. What's the urgent matter that needs to be discussed?" Clint asked. "I heard it was something about robbers."

Before the lawman could respond, the bartender approached the table and held a glass down toward Clint. After glancing at the drink for a fraction of a second, Clint waved it away. "I don't want that."

Even though Clint wasn't looking at the guy, he could hear the scowl on the other man's face when he said, "It's just whiskey."

"I don't want to drink whiskey."

"Then what do you want?"

Clint shrugged and leaned so both elbows were resting on the table. "Something else. Just surprise me."

The barkeep stomped away while muttering something under his breath.

"You're not from around here," the lawman pointed out.

"No, I'm not."

"I'm Marshal Flynt."

"Clint Adams."

Raising an eyebrow, the marshal asked, "Clint Adams, the Gunsmith?"

"That's right."

"Then you're just the sort of man I'd like to talk to."

The barkeep returned with a mug of beer in his hand. Clint heard the angry steps approaching, turned around to look, and then waved him away again. "Try something else."

Baring his teeth as if he meant to bite, the barkeep said, "Tell me what you want!"

"I don't want anything," Clint replied. "If you insist on making me pay for a drink, at least bring me something good." Smirking as the barkeep stormed away again, Clint shifted his eyes back to Flynt. "Better hurry this up, Marshal. I think I'm wearing out my welcome."

"You ever hear of a robber named Laramie Harvey?" Flynt asked.

"That name sounds familiar, but I can't quite put my finger on it."

"He's some bloodthirsty kid that tears through this county and a few surrounding ones with another fella by the name of Chris Jerrison."

Suddenly, Clint snapped his fingers. "Harvey and Chris. Now I know where I heard those names." Seeing the barkeep approach the table with a glass, Clint waited for the man to get close enough and then grimaced and shook his head. The barkeep turned around and walked back to his bar. "A few men tried to steal my horse right before I got to town. They seemed harmless enough."

"Was one of them a black fella?"

Clint studied the lawman for a second before answering. "Yes."

"That'd be them," Flynt grunted with a dismissive wave of his hand. "And don't try to tell me they're harmless. You just said they tried to steal your horse."

"Yeah, but they weren't much of a threat. I suppose they might frighten some women or men that don't have any business riding out on their own, but they weren't much trouble."

"Maybe not for a gunfighter like you, but they're plenty of trouble to the good folks in these parts."

"Then it looks like you've got your work cut out for you, Marshal."

Flynt had no trouble picking up on the emphasis that was given to that last word. "I may be the law around here, but my territory covers a whole lot of miles. The reason I put the word out was to form a posse with the intent of rounding Laramie and his boys up and showing them what's what."

"From what I saw, Laramie was the boy of that group."

"Fine, then why don't you help me track down that boy

and the rest of his group? There's pay in it for you and if you charge extra for killin' those assholes, I can see about payin' that fee as well. It'd be worth it."

"I don't know what you've heard about me," Clint said in the steadiest tone he could manage, "but I'm no hired killer."

"All right. Whatever you call yourself, come along with me and my boys and we'll make it worth your while."

The smugness in the marshal's voice, combined with his slack-jawed smile and piggish eyes, made Clint want to take a swing at the lawman. When Flynt looked across the table at him as though he were looking down into a rat's nest, Clint wanted to bounce the fat man off the floor even more.

Rather than give in to those temptations, Clint took a breath and stood up. "I think I'll pass."

Marshal Flynt twitched as if he'd just witnessed the unthinkable. "What? Why? There's good money to be made."

"I don't need to explain myself. I'll just pass."

All but jumping from his chair, Flynt snapped, "Maybe I did have you pegged wrong. Maybe you're not a gunfighter. Maybe you're an outlaw. That would explain why you don't mind seeing a man like Laramie traipse about as he pleases!"

"Let me ask you something, Marshal. Are these men wanted for murder?"

Settling back as if he'd already won his fight, Flynt replied, "Not as such, but I'm sure they've killed plenty."

"How are you so sure?" Clint asked.

"What the hell difference does it make?"

"The same difference that separates a lynching from a hanging and if you don't know that difference, I sure don't want to ride with you or your men."

Clint started to turn, but almost ran into the barkeep.

Looking down at the glass in the barkeep's hand, Clint said, "Forget the drink. I'll just be on my way."

As he walked out of Tanner Hall, Clint couldn't decide whether the barkeep or the marshal was cussing the loudest.

EIGHT

When Clint walked down Sales Street, he intended on collecting Eclipse and putting Red Water behind him. For the most part, that was a reflection of just how badly Marshal Flynt had ruffled his feathers. By the time he made it to the next corner and was in sight of the stable, Clint's temper had simmered down a bit. It may have been due to the fresh air, or the fact that the stable ahead of him was the same one that he and Gwen had visited the night before.

Either way, Clint was in better spirits when he walked past the corral and stepped into the stable itself. Of course Eclipse was in there waiting for him, but he was more surprised to see another familiar face.

"Oh!" Allie said with a start. "It's you."

Clint nodded and approached her. Allie's hand was still reaching out to rub Eclipse's nose. "It's me, all right," he said. "And that's my horse. Were you expecting me to be gone a bit longer?"

"No, I just . . . that is . . ." Allie stammered.

Watching her fumble about for her next few words, Clint couldn't help but smile. Allie was wearing a simpler dress than the one she'd had on when she'd greeted Clint upon entering town the day before. It was pale yellow with a white apron, which looked freshly bleached.

"Do you remember me?" Clint asked.

"Yes," she replied quickly. Blushing and rubbing her temples, she added, "Mostly, I do. I don't recall your name, though."

"It's Clint."

"I'm—"

"Allie," Clint cut in as he stepped forward to offer his hand. "I heard it from your friend."

"Oh . . . would that be Gwen?"

"It's fair that you don't recall who I am," Clint pointed out, "but you might not tell Gwen that you forgot about her." The only reason he'd said that was to see if he could darken the color in Allie's cheeks. It didn't take long for Clint to realize he'd accomplished that mission.

Trying to hide her reddening face, Allie quickly realized she didn't have enough hands for the job. Rather than turn completely away from him, she cleared her throat and straightened up. "I was a little tipsy last night," she told him. "If I said anything out of line, I apologize."

Clint shook his head. "You don't have anything to apologize for. Certainly nothing worth the effort of tracking me down."

"You say that now, but . . ."

Clint started to feel bad for making her squirm so much, so he let her off the hook. "I've seen many drunks that have plenty to apologize for. The only thing you did was sing a little too loud and stomp a few feet when you danced."

"You saw that, huh?"

"Yeah," Clint replied.

"So your name is Clint?" Allie asked.

"That's right." Since Allie seemed to be stuck in her spot,

Clint stepped up to Eclipse so he could look the stallion over. Not only was the Darley Arabian in good condition, but he seemed reluctant for Allie to stop petting him.

Allie had yet to leave. In fact, she was currently staring at Clint's face as if she were trying to commit every line to memory. "Is there anything else you needed?" he asked.

"No. I suppose not. Did you . . . umm . . . come to town alone?"

"Yes, I did."

"Do you know anyone around here?" Allie asked in a manner that was trying to be casual but was most definitely forced.

"Just Gwen and you," Clint told her. "Why do you ask?"

Allie shrugged her shoulders, shook her head, and chewed on her lower lip all at the same time. "I don't know. I was just making conversation."

"It seems you're not the only one to have trouble in that area. At least you're doing better than the marshal."

Suddenly, Allie's eyes brightened and she no longer looked as if she were about to squirm out of her skin. "You already went to see the marshal?"

"Yeah," Clint grumbled. "He's a real piece of work."

"You talked to him?"

"Yes, I did. Is there something wrong with that?"

"No," Allie sighed. "I just feel foolish . . . again. It seems like I can't do anything but make a fool out of myself when you're around."

Clint pulled in a breath and let it out. Since that didn't do much to help ease his nerves, he took another breath and then asked, "Did I miss something here?"

She shook her head. "No. Someone just came along to let us know that Marshal Flynt was in town and he wanted to see all the men about something important. I saw some of his deputies posted at the end of Sales Street as if they were watching both ends of the town. I asked what the fuss was about and . . ."

Since she was starting to stumble over her words again, Clint said, "And you were told about the outlaws."

"That's right," Allie replied with a nod. "These strangers are supposed to be real dangerous and the marshal is paying a handsome reward for information about them."

"I'm a stranger, so you thought you'd come to see if I was one of the outlaws? That's not exactly a wise plan. If I *was* one of the wanted men, it could have been dangerous for you to confront me."

Averting her eyes from him, she said, "That's why I only came to confront your horse."

"You'd recognize an outlaw by his horse?" Clint asked.

"One of the deputies saw the outlaws' horses. I knew you'd put yours up in this stable, so I came along to get a look."

"Did I pass the test?"

When Allie laughed, it seemed as if she'd finally let go of what had been weighing her down. Not only did her smile seem more genuine, but she even stopped turning away from him. "Yes. You passed. Can I . . . that is, would you mind having lunch with me?"

"I was about to leave town."

Before Clint could say another word, Allie winced as if his answer had truly hurt. Always a sucker when it came to hurt women, Clint quickly added, "But I can put it off for a bit. I did just have breakfast, though."

Immediately regaining her smile, Allie said, "That's fine! I own a little place on Franklin Avenue, just off Sales Street. Come by there when you get hungry and I'll make something for you. It's the least I can do after accusing you of being some sort of criminal."

Clint wanted to tell her she hadn't offended him in the least. In fact, she'd given him a little more information about a few things, but there was no reason to tell her that either. "Lunch sounds good," he said.

Judging by the smile on Allie's face, that was enough. "Good. I'll see you then."

Watching her stroll out of the stable, Clint wondered just how much Gwen had told her about the previous night. Either way, Clint had found enough good qualities in Red Water to wash out the foul taste Tanner Hall had left in his mouth.

NINE

After deciding to stay in Red Water for a little while, Clint had been content to find a saloon far away from Marshal Flynt and a poker game to distract him until lunch. While walking through town, Clint realized that all of Red Water basically branched off Sales Street. Those roads were all avenues and some weren't much more than alleyways. Once he found his way back onto Sales Street, Clint took a look up and down.

Allie had been right. There were armed men posted at either end of the street, men he had to assume were Flynt's deputies. More than that, their positions allowed them to get a good look at who came and went within Red Water. The deputies also must have been able to see anyone approaching or leaving the town's borders.

It was a good way to keep an eye on Red Water while also making it easy to take a shot at anyone they didn't like. Just seeing the men posted in those spots didn't set right with Clint. When he turned his back on the men to head into a saloon, Clint was downright uncomfortable.

Turning to look back at one end of Sales Street, Clint instantly realized why he felt so uncomfortable. One of the deputies was staring straight back at him as though only a few feet instead of a hundred yards separated them.

Despite the knot that was forming in his stomach, Clint put a smile on his face and moseyed toward that end of the street. He kept his steps slow and easy, which still brought him to within a few paces of the deputy fairly quickly.

Seeing the deputy's grip tighten around the rifle he was carrying, Clint raised his hands and said, "I don't want any trouble."

"What is it you do want, mister?" the deputy asked.

"Just out for a walk, is all."

"Yeah? Then keep walkin'."

It seemed this deputy had learned his manners directly from Marshal Flynt. Clint resisted the urge to knock the tough glare from the younger man's face and kept his own smile where it was. "I hear there's trouble about."

The deputy's eyes narrowed a bit as if he were studying Clint even closer. "Could be."

Clint used every bit of acting skill he had, mixed in with a whole lot of bluffing to try to convince the younger man that he was intimidated by him. "There's no trouble from me," he insisted. "I've already been to see the marshal and he told me all about the killers riding through these parts."

Despite the fact that Clint wasn't much of an actor, the deputy was the sort of young man who was anxious to think he could cause someone to shake in their boots. He took to Clint's performance the way a cat laps a saucer of milk. Nodding slightly while shifting his rifle to a more comfortable grip, he said, "They're killers, all right. I'll be on the posse to bring them in."

"Is that why you and the other deputy are watching the street?"

Following Clint's gaze toward the other end of Sales Street, the deputy nodded again. "Them killers might try to come into town for supplies and such. If they come anywhere near here, we'll pick them off."

"That'd make things a hell of a lot easier, wouldn't it?"

"Sure would."

"So . . ." Clint sighed as he drifted even closer to what he really wanted to know. "Who are these men you're after?"

The deputy grinned as if he'd been waiting all day for someone to ask that question. "Real murderous cocksuckers led by a man named Laramie. Him, some known killer named Jerrison, and a black fella have been stealing everything that ain't nailed down."

Clint let out a slow whistle and said, "Sound like real hard cases."

"The worst. They're the sort that would just as soon shoot you as look at you."

"I suppose they'll hang once you get ahold of them."

"If you're set on watching a hanging, I wouldn't hold my breath," the deputy said. "The only thing we intend on dragging back into town is a few carcasses. You want in on the reward, then you'll show up at Dale's."

"Well, then," Clint replied. "It's good to know we got men like you watching over us."

With that, Clint gave a quick wave to the deputy and started walking back down Sales Street. It was a test of his resolve to keep from reacting to the arrogance spewing out of the younger man like pus from an open sore.

TEN

Clint couldn't find a poker game in Red Water, but he didn't have much trouble starting one up. He made the rounds to a few saloons, found his way back to the first one that had struck his fancy, and then broke out a deck of cards. After a few hands of gin with a local and a whole lot of big talk about gambling for big money, Clint was able to pick out a few interested faces among the men leaning against the bar.

Like most saloons, big talk didn't amount to much. After plenty of bragging, the locals clustered around one table and started a boisterous penny-ante game. Clint was just happy to while away a couple of hours and purposely lost a few dollars so the others wouldn't lose interest. When he felt the first grumblings in his belly, Clint played for keeps.

To the locals' credit, they stayed put even after Clint had doubled his money. When Clint finally got up to leave, the other players made him promise to return, but still seemed relieved that he was gone. Before Clint got outside of the saloon, he could overhear the men at the table planning to win their money back at the next game. Clint smirked and made sure to remember the name of the place so he could win some more traveling money before leaving.

It wasn't difficult to find Franklin Avenue. It was one
of the larger branches off Sales Street and one of the only
ones that was wide enough to accommodate a carriage without the wheels scraping against the boardwalk. One such
carriage was parked directly outside the store that Allie had
told him about. Even though he recognized the name from
the one she'd mentioned back at the stable, Clint still wasn't
convinced it was the place he wanted to be.

"Franklin Fixtures," Clint recited. Those were the only
two words on that sign, but he looked around for another
sign just to be sure. What threw him off was the display of
cast iron spigots, pipes, and even a few potbellied stoves in
the window.

Just as Clint started to wonder if the things in the window
were merely decoration, he saw a pair of men shuffle out of
the store carrying a safe to the back of the parked carriage.
Since there were no other places along Franklin Avenue with
a name that was anything close to the store in front of him,
Clint walked around the carriage and to the front door.

Allie stood just inside the place, directing the men with
the safe. She spotted Clint and immediately waved at him.
"There you are! I was just about to have lunch without you."

"What kind of restaurant is this?"

Blinking at Clint and then looking up at the sign directly
over the door, Allie asked, "Restaurant?"

"Yes," Clint replied. "You told me to come here for
lunch?"

"This is called Franklin Fixtures. What kind of food did
you think was served here?"

"I don't know. There's a place in San Antonio called the
Blue Corkboard that serves one hell of a good ham steak.
To this day, I don't know what the hell that name is sup-
posed to mean."

Allie laughed and said, "Well, the fixtures in this name

is just that. I sell just about anything made from iron, even a few bathtubs."

"And what about lunch?" Clint asked.

"I've got extra sandwiches in the back. I thought we could share them."

Studying her through narrowed eyes, Clint said, "Taking pity on a poor traveler on Founder's Day, huh?"

"I don't recall much from last night, but I do recall your face." Allie reached up to run a hand along Clint's cheek and added, "It's just as nice as I remember. If this is a little too forward, then—"

"Nonsense," Clint said before Allie could talk herself out of anything. "But there's got to be a better place to take someone who's new to your town."

"I don't know. I was kind of hoping—"

"What about Dale's?"

Although Allie had been a little flustered before, that condition only got a little worse now. She tried to remedy the situation by looking around and fussing with her hair until it passed. Unfortunately, she was still fussing when she realized it wasn't about to pass. "Umm, Dale's is just a saloon with a . . . it's got a . . . ummm . . ."

"Yes?"

She pulled in another breath, let it out in a huff, and said, "It's got a cathouse on the second floor. It's just a saloon and a cathouse."

"Well," Clint said in a valiant effort to maintain some dignity, "I've heard they serve a great lunch."

ELEVEN

As it turned out, Dale's did serve a good lunch. Judging by the surprised look on Allie's face, that wasn't a normal occurrence. Playing up the ignorance that came along with being new in town, Clint escorted her to Dale's and engaged her in friendly conversation along the way. Once they got within sight of the place, that distraction no longer held up.

Dale's was a wide building with a balcony that extended all the way along the second floor. The balcony was littered with rocking chairs, stools, and anything else the working girls could sit on that gave the folks in the street a good look up their skirts. All Clint could see was a bunch of slips and ruffles, but that didn't calm Allie's nerves very much.

"Looks busy," Clint said.

"Yes, maybe this wasn't such a good idea."

Clint stopped and took hold of her shoulders so he could turn her back to Dale's. "Lunch is my treat," he said. "I'd really like to sit down with you, but I'd also really like to be inside that place." Seeing the discomfort spread across Allie's face, Clint quickly added, "And not because of the entertainment inside."

"Entertainment. That's one word for it."

"Marshal Flynt is going to be gathering some men here and I want to get a look at what they're doing."

Turning around to look at a plump redhead leaning over the balcony, Allie smirked and said, "I think I can tell you what they'll be doing."

"Well, I'm not interested in that. Marshal Flynt and his deputies are forming a posse. You remember all that talk spread around town this morning?"

"You mean about those outlaws?"

"That's right," Clint said.

"Are you going to join the posse? If so, you don't need me to—"

Clint shook his head. "I started off on the wrong foot here. I thought Flynt and his men were just meeting in a saloon or some restaurant to discuss the posse and I figured I could overhear something once we got here."

"So you don't really want to have lunch with me?" Allie asked.

"I do, but I figure being there with you won't make it seem like I am there to be in the posse. I am hoping Flynt doesn't notice us at all, so I can just get a look at how many men are with him and what sort of men they are."

Allie sighed and lowered her head. "I suppose that's good to know before I start talking like a fool without you even listening to me."

Placing his finger under Allie's chin, Clint lifted her face so she had no choice but to look at him. "I didn't know what this place was and I made the suggestion on a whim. No need to read any more into it than that. If you don't want to come with me, that's fine, but I'd still like to see you."

Either Allie was overcome by Clint's charm or she'd caught a whiff of chicken being cooked inside Dale's. The chicken smelled so good that Clint put his money on it being the deciding factor. Whatever the reason, she nodded and turned toward the front door.

"Fine," she said. "But I'm taking you up on your offer to pay."

Clint offered her his arm and she took it.

Once they were inside, it was easy enough to forget the primary source of Dale's revenue. It was late afternoon and the working girls were currently busying themselves by carrying plates of chicken and pitchers of water to the tables scattered throughout the main room. A piano played a lively tune in the corner, and the stage was empty and mostly covered by a curtain.

During the first round of chicken, Allie talked about her fixture business and the trials that came along with setting up a shop in a place like Red Water.

"What about that safe?" Clint asked. "That didn't look like any spigot I've ever seen."

"That was a special order," she said. "It's for a bank in Topeka. They ordered three of them and that's the first."

"Aren't there . . . I don't know . . . safe companies for that sort of thing?"

"Sure, but I can beat their prices," Allie said as if she were sweet-talking Clint into another sale. "A few months ago, I hired a man who specializes in shaping iron."

"You mean a blacksmith?"

"Blacksmiths work on horseshoes and railroad ties," she corrected. "What Sven does is art by comparison. He can take a slab of ore and shape it into something beautiful. He can even make little things like gears and tumblers."

Clint chuckled and tossed a chicken bone onto his plate. "You don't do a lot of work in that area, do you?"

"I appreciate the craftsmanship," she said defensively, "but I just sell it. I also know good work when I see it. I'm the one who talked him into building safes."

"Sven never built a safe before?"

Allie's brow furrowed, but the scowl on her face was still good-natured enough. "I talked him into building safes for *me*," she clarified. "I also managed to get several banks interested enough to make special orders. He should have enough to retire inside of a year."

"That is pretty impressive," Clint said through a mouthful of potatoes.

"What about you?" she asked. "What do you do to earn your keep?"

"I'm a gunsmith."

Her eyes widening to the size of silver dollars, she gasped, "Really? I could put you to work. Do you know how much there is to be made by giving a little healthy competition to the bigger businesses from places like Wichita and Dodge City or even New York?"

Sensing that he was about to be put through the wringer until he caved in to Allie's proposal, Clint was more than happy to see Marshal Flynt and a few others stroll in through the front door. "I don't mean to be rude, Allie, but . . ."

She turned around, spotted the lawmen, and nodded. "Of course. You've got some spying to do."

TWELVE

Marshal Flynt must have been a generous spender at Dale's. Clint gathered as much by watching how the working girls swarmed around him and his men like flies around a wet pile of sugar. They cooed and rubbed against him so much that Clint barely had to do anything to go unnoticed. It was all Flynt could do to pay attention to the men who wanted to see him.

"Any of you men that want to sign on for the posse," Flynt announced, "just write your name down here."

To the marshal's left was a deputy sitting at a table where an open book was displayed like a hotel's register.

Dale's had filled up a bit since the lawmen's arrival, and one of the men clustered around Flynt asked, "What's the pay?"

Flynt smirked like a snake-oil salesman. "So glad you asked. There's a reward posted for Laramie and his men of three hundred dollars a head. I am personally adding another three hundred on top of that if the job gets done sooner rather than later."

"How much sooner?"

"No more than a week. After that, these outlaws will

catch wind that we're after them and go hide in a hole somewhere while we chase our tails. If that happens, I call the search off, find some more capable men, and start again when I figure out where they went."

"Won't they know we're after them the moment we start chasing them down?" the same man asked.

Clint had to smile a bit, since this one fellow in the crowd was asking most of the questions that were coming to his own mind. The marshal, on the other hand, wasn't so delighted.

"You don't want to come, then don't sign." Flynt sneered.

The man who'd been asking the questions was a fellow in his early forties with a bit more meat on his bones than the rest. He shifted in his seat and looked around to the other locals around him. There were enough friendly faces in Dale's to give him the confidence to say, "We didn't just come here to sign. We were told you'd tell us why risking our necks on this posse would be such a good idea."

"Aren't you men willing to do your civic duty and lend a hand to the law when it's needed?" Flynt asked.

There was a span of silence that even weighed heavy on Clint's shoulders. Finally, the man with the questions replied, "Ain't none of us been robbed by these outlaws. Fact is, I don't know anyone that's even seen 'em."

"All right then," Flynt snapped as he slapped his hand flat against the table hard enough to make the book jump. "We'll just wait for these murderers to ride through town, rape a few of our women, kill a couple of you, and set a few fires! How'd you like that?"

Those words were like a cold slap across the face of every man in Dale's. There was, however, one exception.

"Let's not get carried away, here, Marshal," Clint said from his seat.

Flynt squinted at the far side of the room and quickly

picked Clint out. "So you decided to show up after all, huh, Adams?"

"That's right, and I—"

Jabbing a finger toward Clint, the marshal bellowed, "This here is Clint Adams. The Gunsmith! Maybe some of you have heard of him."

Judging by the mixed reaction among the men, a scant few of them had.

Completely unaffected by the majority of men who didn't seem to know Clint from Abraham Lincoln, Marshal Flynt said, "He's seen Laramie and his boys no more than a day's ride from town! And that was yesterday, so they're probably even closer by now!"

The man who'd been grilling the marshal with his earlier questions shifted in his chair until he could get a better look at Clint. "That true?" he asked.

"I don't really know where they were headed," Clint replied. "All I know is that they were after my horse."

"You see?" Flynt cut in. "They're horse thieves! That's a hanging offense!"

"But," Clint added, "they didn't get my horse. They couldn't even get the drop on me at all and I bet they'd have trouble getting the drop on anyone in this room. The men I saw match your description, Marshal. The one who you said leads them, Laramie I think you called him . . ."

"That's right."

"He's a kid. Still wet behind the ears and shooting his mouth off more than his gun. The other men weren't a whole lot worse."

"You know that for a fact?" Marshal Flynt asked.

"From what I saw . . . yeah. I crawled circles around them for a lark and then left them in the dust once I got to my horse." Clint looked around at the other men and told them, "There's got to be more dangerous men in this room."

"You're damn right there are," the marshal said proudly. "That's why we're the men to bring them in."

"You're forming a lynch mob," Clint said once he was looking straight into the marshal's eyes. "Your own deputies are already planning a funeral for a bunch of troublemaking owlhoots. What's your hurry to kill them?"

Marshal Flynt didn't avert his eyes in the slightest as he reached under his coat and drew something that had been hidden until that moment. Although all the men gathered in front of him were anxious to see what the marshal had, Clint couldn't help but inch his hand a little closer to his holster.

Extending his arm to reveal a piece of folded paper the way a magician might reveal a card plucked from a stacked deck, Flynt opened up a freshly printed reward notice. "There!" he proclaimed as he showed the wanted poster for all to see. "'Laramie' Harvey Layton, Chris Jerrison, and that black fella are all wanted men. Dead or alive!"

Clint leaned a bit closer to get a look at the hand-drawn likenesses of the outlaws. Sure enough, there was no name under the black man's picture.

"It says right there, these men are wanted criminals with a death sentence hanging over their heads," Flynt bellowed. "I need a group of men to go after them before they get close enough to do any damage to this good town or any others nearby. The reward will be paid to anyone that nabs these desperadoes and I'll pay the bonus upon completion of the task."

"Where's the bonus coming from?"

Even Clint was surprised to hear the question spoken by the woman directly beside him. When he looked at Allie, he saw her raise her eyebrows and wait patiently for a reply.

"Well, miss," Flynt told her. "The money comes from a pool of concerned business owners."

"I'm a business owner," she said. "I never heard a thing about it."

"Well, it's genuine." With that, Flynt reached into his pocket again to remove a bundle of money. Slamming the stack of bills onto the table, Flynt declared, "And there it is! Any man wants to do his duty as well as claim some of the reward for their own, just sign up."

No more announcements were needed. More than half the men in front of Flynt stood and walked over to sign the book. The other half seemed to be pondering that very same thing.

When Clint took a step forward, he felt Allie touch his arm. "Where are you going?" she asked.

"Where else?" Clint told her. "I'm going to sign that book."

THIRTEEN

After Clint had written his name in Flynt's book, he walked back to find Allie standing in her spot with a puzzled look on her face. He took her arm and escorted her out of Dale's without a word passing between them. By the time they reached the street, however, Allie found plenty of words to throw at him.

"What was that about?" she asked.

Clint blinked with exaggerated confusion. "What do you mean?"

"You sounded like you were dragging the marshal over the coals. Before long, I was starting to wonder if Flynt had a grudge against those outlaws. From what you said, you didn't think there was any need for a posse." The more she said, the more trouble Allie had keeping her focus. "You even told everyone that—"

"I know what I said," Clint interrupted before she could whip herself into even more of a tizzy. "Everything about those horse thieves was true. Laramie is just some kid who barely knows his way around a pistol and I have a real difficult time believing his gang was any sort of terror that needs a bloodthirsty posse set on their tails."

Allie blinked and waited for a few seconds. Before too long, all she could do was blink again. "That really didn't straighten anything out for me. Was this another one of your quick, peculiar decisions?"

More men were streaming out of Dale's. For the most part, they looked like the men who had been there to listen to Flynt's proposal. Upon spotting one of Flynt's deputies, Clint tightened his arm around Allie's and led her down the street as if he were accompanying her to that night's Founder's Day celebration.

"I've never been good at sitting back and letting lynch mobs tear a man down," he explained. "No matter how much some men deserve it, the law has plenty of ways to make a man pay for what he's done. If a group of armed men allow themselves to be led by the likes of that marshal back there, they'll be a hell of a lot more dangerous than most outlaw gangs."

"You sound like you know something on the subject," Allie said warily.

"I've seen more than my share of blood and I won't stand aside so more can be spilled on the word of a liar like Flynt."

"You think Flynt is a liar?"

Once Clint said those words, he instantly regretted it— not because his words were out of line, but because he knew that some folks tended to defend their lawmen before they would side with a stranger. Since Allie seemed more concerned than offended, he guessed that Flynt's reputation wasn't exactly sterling to begin with.

"I can't say for certain he's lying," Clint explained, "but I know he's hiding something. I'd stake my life on that much."

Allie nodded and fell into step with Clint. Already, there was less tension in her shoulders than there had been a few minutes ago. "Nobody around here thinks too much about Flynt, but he usually doesn't spend a lot of time in Red Water to make it worth the trouble of raising a fuss."

"Was he duly appointed to his office?"

"More or less," she said with a shrug. "The marshal before him used to make the rounds between here and other towns pretty regularly. When he stepped down, Flynt took his place. Things have never been too wild around here, so all he's ever needed to do is settle some disputes or chase away some rowdy cowboys every so often. What do you think he's doing with this posse of his?"

"To be honest, I think he's putting together enough gunhands to kill these three men and cut off more than his share of the reward," Clint told her. "Those notices looked fresh, so they could have been printed up by him any way he pleased."

"Why would he do that?"

"The reward could be larger, so he could pay off a smaller amount and keep some for himself. There could be money on those men's heads offered by any number of unsavory sources and Flynt might get an edge on any bounty hunter by forming a legal posse. Having the law on your side makes it a whole lot easier to fire a gun without a proper explanation."

Chuckling uncomfortably, Allie said, "I never thought of anything like that."

"Because you're not a swindler or a killer. Do me a favor, though."

"Depends on what it is," she replied with a crooked grin.

"Turn down this street and walk away from me. If you hear any shooting, just get away and don't come back."

That got rid of Allie's smile real quickly.

FOURTEEN

Clint had glanced back at Dale's every so often as soon as he'd noticed that a few men were following him. There was a certain way armed men walked when they intended on putting their guns to use. There was a look in their eyes that could be seen just as well with a quick glance as it could when there was time to study.

Clint picked up on these things easily, and he knew his suspicions were confirmed when the men increased their speed to catch up to him and Allie. That's when he'd told her to part ways and not look back.

To her credit, Allie seemed confused but still followed Clint's request. At first, she'd actually seemed grateful for a quick excuse to leave him and get back to her normal life. After taking a few steps, she'd decided to stop and turn around anyway. She was just in time to watch Clint turn around to face the three men who'd been chasing after him.

"Can I help you gentlemen?" Clint asked as he planted his feet and let his arms hang down loosely at his sides.

Two of the men wore deputy badges pinned to their shirts. One of the deputies was the same man Clint had spoken to before meeting Allie for lunch. The deputy was still armed, but looked more perturbed than when he'd been guarding the end of Sales Street.

The second deputy was a little taller than Clint and had a head full of bright red hair that was parted neatly down the middle. His eyes were narrowed into slits and his hand hung within easy reach of a .44 at his hip. Judging by the bulge under his jacket, the deputy was carrying some iron under there as well.

The third man wasn't wearing a badge, but he'd been one of the more enthusiastic members of the group listening to Flynt's speech back at Dale's. His right fist was wrapped around a thick piece of lumber that was roughly the length of an ax handle, which he slapped menacingly against his other palm.

"Yeah," the tall redheaded deputy replied. "You can tell us what you mean by signing on for the posse when you had nothing but bullshit to say to the marshal's face."

"Wasn't the purpose of that meeting to ask questions?" Clint said. "Isn't that all I did?"

Coming to a stop less than a foot or two in front of Clint, the redhead stared down at him to make sure everyone knew who was bigger than whom. "Now we got some questions for you. Think you'll be willing to answer them, or should we just cross your name off the list?"

"I don't mind answering—"

"Good," the redhead cut in. "Why don't you let Frank and Arvin here show you to a spot where we can talk?"

Clint could feel the other two men closing in on him like a vise. Keeping his eyes on the redhead, he said, "I'm comfortable where I am."

"Folks around here have been distressed enough. If you want to ride with the law, you'll have to respect how we do things."

"All right. Lead the way."

The redhead nodded, which was the signal for the other two to grab one of Clint's arms. Rather than pull away at the first chance he got, Clint allowed himself to be led to the cramped space between a nearby general store and saddle shop. That way, he could get a feel for the strength of the two men while letting them get comfortable in the knowledge that they had the upper hand.

Clint dug his heels into the dirt as soon as he realized the men intended on dragging him around back of the stores and out of sight completely. "This is far enough," he said. "What did you want to ask me?"

Frank and Arvin tried to keep pulling Clint along, but stopped when they saw a subtle nod from the redhead.

"Sounds to me like you know those outlaws pretty damn well," the redheaded deputy said. "I'd like to know why that is."

"I told you, they tried to steal my horse."

"And tell me again why you seem to be on their side after they tried to steal your horse."

"I'm not," Clint said. "Now why don't you tell me why you and your men decided to drag me off the street when I signed on to help you."

The redhead leaned in close enough for Clint to smell what the other man had had for breakfast. "We don't want the help of some chickenshit tenderfoot with a loud mouth."

"You've got one second to take that back," Clint warned.

"Or what?" the redhead scoffed. "You'll—"

Having been generous with the amount of time he'd actually given the deputy, Clint wasn't about to continue that generosity any further. Snapping one leg up, he drove his knee into the redhead's stomach with enough force to double him over. Clint then cinched his right arm around the arm of the deputy holding him on that side, while pulling his left straight out of Arvin's grasp.

Arvin wasn't about to let go easily, so Clint snapped his boot into his shin. Clint's heel landed with a solid crack and put an ugly wince onto Arvin's face. After that, the posse member couldn't let go of him fast enough.

The redhead was a tough fellow, because he was already recovering from Clint's initial blow. As soon as he straightened up, however, the redhead was knocked aside by the second deputy. Clint twisted his entire body around so his hip was against Frank's midsection. Once he had a good pivot point working in his favor, Clint swung Frank into the redhead as if he were tossing a sack of grain against a wall.

Allowing the men to catch their breath, Clint told them, "You had that coming for flapping your gums so recklessly. Since we're working together, we can call it even."

The redhead shoved the other two away from him so he could square his shoulders to Clint. "We ain't about to work together," he snarled. "And we sure as hell didn't bring you here to call it even."

Upon getting a quick nod from the redhead, Frank snapped a fist at Clint with just enough speed for the punch to land. Clint tensed for it and turned so the deputy's knuckles slammed against muscle rather than ribs. Before Frank could deliver a follow-up punch, Clint sent a jab into Frank's face. The fast punch hit him in the mouth, snapped his head back, and sent him staggering a few steps.

Clint wasn't able to do anything before Arvin came at him from the side. The posse member lowered his shoulder and ran at Clint like a bull. Turning toward Arvin, Clint felt the incoming shoulder brush against him as he kept on turning. Once he'd moved enough for Arvin to pass by him, Clint gave him a quick punch in the ribs to take with him. Arvin let out a grunt and did his best to skid to a stop.

When Clint faced the redhead again, he saw the deputy

reach for the gun holstered at his side. In a flicker of motion, Clint drew his modified Colt and aimed it at the deputy.

"Last chance to call it even," Clint said. "What do you say?"

Since the redhead was caught with his .44 only halfway out of its holster, he opened his hand to let it drop back in place. "Fine, but you've been warned. You try to work against this posse and you'll be strung up right alongside Laramie and them other two."

Clint nodded and stepped back so he could keep all three men in his sights. "I'll be sure to keep that in mind. You fellows give my best to Marshal Flynt."

The men grumbled plenty of foul words as Clint headed for the street, but they made sure to keep their voices low enough to stay out of trouble.

FIFTEEN

Clint left the alley in a rush, but wasn't about to give the three men the pleasure of thinking they'd scared him out. He kept his steps purposeful and got away without running. Once he was a ways down the street, he found a spot on the boardwalk, leaned against a post, and kept his eyes open.

Frank emerged first. The deputy looked up and down the street a few times before realizing he was drawing plenty of attention on his own. He holstered his pistol and motioned for the men behind him to do the same. After that, Arvin and the redhead stepped out.

Arvin was more nervous than the other two combined. Clint could tell that much even with a good portion of the street between them. The redhead may or may not have spotted Clint, but he obviously knew it was too late to rekindle any more trouble without possibly turning things into a full shooting war. Judging by the way he scolded the other two men, Clint guessed the redhead was saying as much right now.

Just to be safe, Clint lowered his head so his hat covered most of his face. There were enough other people on the street around him to keep him hidden until the three men walked back toward Dale's.

"What was the meaning of that?" Allie asked as she practically leaped at Clint from a doorway.

Clint couldn't help but jump. "Jesus! Where were you hiding?"

"I wasn't far enough away to keep from noticing that fight you had back there. Are you all right?"

"I'm fine."

"No, you're not," she said as she reached out to fuss with his face and shirt. "You're all rumpled and . . . are you bleeding?"

Gently moving her hands away from him, Clint turned and wrapped an arm around Allie to move her along with him. "I'm trying not to draw any attention here, and you're not helping."

"Then maybe I should just run along and have a word with the marshal. Perhaps he'd like to know you were attacking his men."

"You truly think that?" Clint asked.

"With all the nonsense you've been saying and doing, I hardly know what to think."

Allie wasn't a pivotal part of anything Clint was doing. He knew he could leave her where she stood and was fairly confident she wouldn't try to get him into any trouble with the law. What he didn't like, however, was the anger that was spreading across her face like a brushfire. She was much too pretty to be left so angry.

"Sorry about all of this," he told her. "I truly am. Sometimes I kind of get pulled into these things."

"From where I'm standing, you didn't get pulled into anything. It looked to me like you walked in all by yourself."

"That's fair enough."

Although she worked to stay mad, Allie was unable to

maintain the stern frown that she'd been wearing only a few moments ago. Instead, she lowered her voice and told him, "If Marshal Flynt wasn't such a shifty-eyed pig, I would've kept walking when you told me to."

"But you didn't."

"No. I guess I didn't."

"Why's that?" Clint asked.

"Because," Allie replied, "there's one more night of Founder's Day to celebrate and I don't want to do it alone."

"Those must have been some founders to get a day that lasts for two."

"Try four," she corrected. "To be honest, this town just sort of carries on to carry on. I doubt more than a few of the old-timers can actually name one of the founders."

"I was planning on looking into Flynt's posse," Clint said.

"You should have time. The music won't even get started for another few hours."

Clint's intention had been to get out of town and move along. That had been his intention for some time and, like the times before it, something came along to push that intention toward the back of his head.

There was an unmistakable gleam in Allie's eye that told him she truly wanted him to stay for a dance. And after dancing, there was always more to do. Suddenly, something else came to mind.

"What about Gwen?" he asked. "She took up most of my dancing time the other night."

"It was more than that, from what I hear," Allie replied with a knowing, and approving, smirk.

Now there was no chance of Clint leaving before he saw the night through.

SIXTEEN

Allie had her shop to tend to and Gwen was nowhere to be found, so Clint was able to deal with his own business for the rest of the day. As it turned out, his business didn't consist of much more than finding a spot across from Dale's and watching men drift in and out of the place. Marshal Flynt had set up shop inside and only stuck his nose out for the occasional breath before getting back to his table.

Once in a while, Clint peeked through the window to make sure the lawmen hadn't slipped out through some back door. As early evening came along, Clint grew tired of lurking and decided to have a beer. He could think of a lot better places than Dale's, but none of those places made him feel like the center of attention.

The second he walked inside, most of the people at Dale's were looking him over. Flynt and the other lawmen stared him down as if Clint's face were on the wanted posters, while the bartender didn't try to hide the fact that he was reaching below the bar for some sort of weapon. Before any threats could be made, Clint stole the barkeep's thunder by striding up to the bar and proclaiming, "I'll have a beer."

"You'll pay for it here and now," the barkeep warned. "I ain't about to run back and forth."

"Of course," Clint said. "That's the policy. It's written right there on the sign."

Even though the bartender had looked ready to take a swing at Clint before, those words nearly brought him over the top of the bar to lunge at Clint's throat. Instead, he quickly filled a glass, slammed it on the bar so half of it spilled onto the floor, and then charged him full price. Clint took the beer and casually walked over to the table where the lawmen were holding court.

"You got some nerve showing your face around here." Flynt grunted.

"Why?" Clint asked. "You intend on throwing me in jail for not allowing your men to drag me off the street and beat me to a pulp?"

Flynt's eyes narrowed, making his fleshy face seem even more piggish. "What do you want, Adams?"

"I want to know when we're leaving. I am still on the posse, right?"

"I figured that was some sort of joke."

Clint pulled in a breath and let it out as a sigh. Leaning down a bit, he dropped his voice and said, "A man in my line of work can't afford to be talked about like I'm just some dreg who takes money for pulling a trigger. Every saloon is full of men who would take a shot at me the minute they thought I could be pushed around so easily. Your men went too far and they got what they deserved as well. I'm here now to talk to you man to man."

It took a few moments, but Flynt grunted to the deputies surrounding him and they found somewhere else to be. He then motioned to one of the free chairs and waited for Clint to sit down before grumbling, "But what you said about them outlaws . . ."

"What did you expect me to say? That I was trembling at the thought of someone like Laramie setting his sights on me? If I said anything else about them, I'd have other gunmen looking me up the minute I stepped out that door. Surely, a man like you knows this sort of thing."

Marshal Flynt was confused. That much could be seen on his face, which was just fine by Clint. After all, Clint had specifically mixed a bunch of nonsense in with enough compliments to Flynt's supposed toughness to completely snow the lawman.

Rather than admit to his confusion or ask Clint to explain himself any more, the marshal accepted the double-talk with half a grin. "Yeah," he said. "I know plenty about that sort of thing. Just like you should know I couldn't sit back and let you call me out like that in my own town."

Clint nodded. "I know. That's why I didn't kill any of those deputies you sent out for me. It's also why I'd still like to ride with your posse."

"You do?"

"I have a reputation to uphold, but your money spends just as well as anyone else's. I also think you know just as well as I do that my services are worth a bit more than what you're paying the rest of these locals."

Now that he was back on his own ground, Flynt leaned in his rickety chair like a king reclining on his throne. "Why should I do that?"

"Because," Clint replied simply, "I can lead you to these men in half the time."

"You ain't known as a tracker."

"You've heard plenty about me."

"Yeah," Flynt replied. "I have."

"Men in saloons gossip plenty about folks like me. As you can see, I do plenty to make sure everything about me isn't so widely known. That's what keeps someone like me alive while others like Laramie wind up on wanted notices or under a few feet of dirt."

Clint was truly getting a feel for what sort of double-talk the marshal wanted to hear and what would confuse him just enough to suit Clint's purposes. Flynt's eyes clouded over a bit, but he kept nodding as if he knew exactly what Clint was talking about. If that truly was the case, he'd already know that Clint was stringing together half-truths with chunks of manure as he went along.

"I can pay you twice the going rate," Flynt said, "but you'll have to do more work."

"I'll track those outlaws and make sure you men get pointed in the right direction."

"If we find them, I expect you to put that famous gun of yours to work as well," Flynt demanded.

"You're the boss. Just to be clear," Clint added as a way to maintain the picture he'd put into the lawman's head, "I don't want to hear any talk about you shoving me around or keeping me in line. I'll take orders from you, but—"

Flynt cut him off by using his fingers to turn an imaginary key over his liver lips. "This arrangement is between us," he grumbled.

"When does the posse leave?"

"First light, tomorrow morning. None of the locals would leave before Founder's Day was over anyhow. Have a good time, but not too good."

Standing up, Clint nodded and said, "I'll just have to see about that."

SEVENTEEN

Before Clint had to wonder where he might get supper that night, he could smell beef being cooked someplace just outside the window of his rented room. Opening the window and leaning outside, Clint quickly realized the entire street was filled with the inviting scent, which emanated from a long table set beneath the Founder's Day banner.

Clint threw on a nicer shirt and gave his boots a once-over before strolling down to the festivities. Soon after he'd tracked down the food piled onto the table, he spotted Allie waving to him from across the street. She wore a black dress accented by white ribbons and walked with just enough of a strut to show she was aware of how well the dress hugged her figure.

"Glad to see you're still here," she said as she stepped up beside him and took a clean plate from the pile at the end of the table. Glancing at Clint's face, she added, "And no more bruises, I see."

"Not yet anyway," Clint chided.

"So you're still going along with that posse?"

Busying himself with the ample selection of meat, vegetables, and other side dishes, he replied, "That's the plan."

"Correct me if I'm wrong, but it looked like those were the marshal's men who pulled you off the street."

"They were. Marshal Flynt and I have come to an understanding." Seeing the puzzled expression on her face, Clint leaned in close to her ear and added, "I blew enough smoke for him to come around to my way of thinking."

Allie giggled and scooped a bit of food onto her own plate. "How much smoke are you talking about?"

"Just enough to make him think he was still the big, tough lawman and I'm the hired gun he was after in the first place."

"Maybe you should have used some of that smoke earlier. It could have saved you a bruise or two."

"It took me a while to make sure I wanted to go through the trouble."

"Tell me again," Allie said, "why you want to go through the trouble now."

Having reached the end of the table, Clint waited for her to finish picking out what she wanted. Even after accepting some dishes offered by the locals who'd made them for the celebration, Allie's plate was piled less than half as high as Clint's. Rather than stop at the spot where Clint waited, Allie led the way to a pair of chairs set up beneath a nearby tree.

"Something's not right with that marshal," Clint said after they'd both sat down.

"I could have told you that," she replied. "He's always been a foul-mouthed idiot."

"It's more than that. There's something I'm missing and it's driving me crazy."

"Are you always so tenacious?"

"Yeah," Clint admitted with a shrug. "It tends to get me into a lot of tight spots, but I can't just step aside when I might be able to do something to help."

"Who are you helping?"

Clint looked down at his plate, picked up a warm biscuit, and took a bite. Once his mouth wasn't so full, he said, "I haven't quite decided yet. If this Laramie fellow is just some wayward kid who the marshal wants to string up for some reason of his own, I can prevent that from happening. If those outlaws truly are half as bad as folks are saying, then I can help with that, too.

"I've ridden along with more posses than I can count," Clint continued. "This one just feels . . . wrong. Whether it is or isn't, I can add something to the mix."

"And," Allie declared as she pointed a carrot stick at him, "you just can't abide something going on without you getting your hands in it."

"I'd rather think it was something more that that, but you might be onto something there."

"I know I am," she said proudly. "I could recognize it."

"Have you known other men like me?"

She cheerfully shook her head and told him, "No, but both of my grandmothers were fussy busybodies and they had the same problem."

Clint looked at her for a few seconds and then broke out laughing. Rather than discus the matter any further, he shifted the conversation to other subjects ranging from the state of Allie's fixture shop to the sort of trouble her friend Gwen liked to get herself into.

Scattered throughout the crowd were a few of Flynt's deputies and several men who had signed on to the posse. With so much of the posse in plain sight, Clint allowed himself to relax and enjoy the night without worrying about the lawmen riding off without him. Even after the music and dancing got started, Marshal Flynt's booming, drunken voice could be heard from nearly anywhere in town.

Clint divided his time between piling food onto his plate and dancing enough to make an appetite for another helping.

Allie kicked up her heels and started sipping wine as soon as she'd had her dessert. From there, she was either being spun around by Clint in the middle of the other dancing couples or twirling over to some friend of hers who waited with open arms. Clint was surprised to find someone waiting for him as well.

"You didn't forget about me, did you?" Gwen asked.

Clint's eyes reflexively twitched to where Allie was dancing. "Not at all," he replied. "I just figured—"

"You figured I'd find somewhere else to be while you romanced my friend," she said as she sidled her way over to him without losing a step to the beat of the music.

"That's not it at all," Clint replied. He did his best to keep his voice steady, but it was getting more and more difficult as Gwen placed her hands on his hips and writhed against him. "A lot's happened since I've been here."

"It's only been a day."

"Feels a lot longer than that."

Suddenly, Gwen reached between Clint's legs. "It is a lot longer, but I think you'll need some coaxing to get there."

Clint smiled, but soon noticed that Allie was making her way over to him. He tried to turn so Gwen couldn't maintain her grip, but she moved right along with him. Finally, Clint positioned himself so that he was facing Allie while Gwen had her back to Allie.

"There's Allie now," Clint said, hoping Gwen might decide to back up on her own.

Keeping one hand on Clint's crotch, Gwen looked over her shoulder and used her free hand to wave.

Allie walked right over to them and acknowledged Gwen with a tip of the glass she was holding. "You two found each other again, I see."

"Actually," Clint replied, "we were just mentioning that—"

"Tell you what," Allie interrupted. "Why don't the both of you come where I can talk to you without so much noise?"

Clint shook his head. "No need for that. We're just having fun."

Glancing down to where Gwen's other hand was, Allie said, "I just bet you are. Come along with me. You'll want to hear this."

Gwen shrugged and turned to follow her friend. Considering where he was being held, Clint didn't have much choice but to follow.

EIGHTEEN

Between trying to keep up with Gwen and trying not to look like he was being led by a very delicate leash, Clint didn't have any idea where he was going. He doubted he was in too hot water, since both women seemed pleasant enough whenever they looked back to check on him. They didn't have any weapons in their hands, so he doubted he was being set up for anything too dangerous. Once he was dragged through a narrow doorway just off the street, however, Clint noticed a definite change in Allie's demeanor.

"So you think you can just ride into town and treat us how you please?" Allie asked.

Clint could see lengths of brass railings and shiny new spigots hanging here and there on the walls. "We're at your shop?"

"That's right. It's closed up, so nobody's going to find you."

"Besides," Gwen added, "it's not like anyone's really looking for you anyhow."

"What's this about?" Clint asked.

Allie rushed forward with enough speed to make Clint's

hand reflexively jump to the gun at his side. He didn't clear leather, but he kept his palm resting against the grip.

Allie drew in a quick breath as she looked down to see the pistol that had almost been drawn. "What's the matter, Clint? You nervous?"

"Not yet."

"Well, you should be," Gwen whispered into Clint's ear. "After what you did to me. Did you think I wouldn't tell my friend about what happened?"

"And then you were acting so cordial with me," Allie purred into his other ear. "Did you think you could have us both?"

Clint stood perfectly still. Although he was a little uneasy about where the conversation could be headed, he couldn't deny what the women's warm breath on his skin was doing to him. When he spoke again, he knew he had to pick his words very carefully. All he could come up with was, "No?"

Allie's lip curled into a subtle pout. "You didn't? That's a shame."

Taking that as an invitation, Clint leaned over to plant a kiss on Allie's lips. She was surprised for a second, but quickly gave in to his advance by pressing her body against him. He slipped his tongue into her mouth, which brought a soft moan from the back of Allie's throat.

At first, Clint could only feel Allie's hands sifting through his hair and rubbing against his chest. Soon, he could feel another set of hands slowly massaging his shoulders and then raking down along his back.

"Save some for me," Gwen said.

Clint turned toward the sound of Gwen's voice to find her anxiously awaiting him. Before he could kiss her, she practically devoured him with a kiss of her own. Compared to Allie's soft, eager lips, Gwen's were more urgent and her tongue wrapped around his own as if she'd been starving for him ever since they'd last been together.

When Clint was finally able to break away long enough to catch his breath, he looked back and forth between the two women. "I've got to admit. I wasn't expecting this."

Allie smiled warmly and eased the top of her dress down to reveal her breasts. Large, dark nipples capped the delicate flesh. As she slid her dress down even farther, Allie leaned her head back to fully savor the way the material brushed against her naked skin. After a few more wriggles, she was able to drop most of her clothing to a pile around her feet. That left her only wearing stockings held up by a lacy garter. "Well, you'd better get used to the idea," she told him. "Because it's too late to go back now."

Clint had no intention of going back. On the contrary, he was aching to go forward. His erection strained against his jeans as he reached out to wrap his hands around Allie's waist. The instant he pulled her even closer to him, she writhed against the bulge in his crotch and made a contented moaning sound that he could barely hear.

"Let's just see what all the fuss was about," Allie whispered. She then unbuckled his belt and pulled his jeans open so she could reach inside. By the time Allie had slipped her fingers around the shaft of his cock, Gwen was tugging his jeans all the way down.

"Didn't I tell you?" Gwen teased.

"You two talked about a whole lot when I wasn't around," Clint said.

"Of course," Allie replied. "But I wanted to see for myself." Keeping hold of him, she lowered herself to her knees and placed her lips around the tip of his penis. Allie moved her head forward so his rigid member was enveloped by her mouth until she'd taken nearly every last inch of him inside.

Clint let out a long breath as he felt Allie's tongue go to work on him. Just when he'd collected himself, he looked over to see Gwen staring straight at him. She wore a wicked smile and didn't get a chance to say a word before Clint reached out for her.

Allie's head bobbed back and forth as she sucked him like a stick of candy. Meanwhile, Clint had grabbed Gwen by the back of the head so he could give her a powerful kiss. He figured by the look in her eyes that she was a wild one and he was proven right when Gwen responded to his kiss. Her tongue wrestled with his while Allie hungrily sucked him.

"All right," Clint said. "Let's see if I can give you both something to talk about after I'm gone."

He eased back from Allie's face and helped her to her feet. Then Clint took hold of Gwen and reached up under her skirts to pull down her undergarments. She wasn't wearing much beneath her dress, but what she did have on ripped all too easily when Clint got ahold of it. Even though he hadn't meant to tear the clothing, Clint saw a definite spark in Gwen's eyes when she heard the tearing of fabric. He reached through the shredded material and found the thatch of hair between her legs that was every bit as soft and curly as the hair on her head.

Gwen's pussy was warm and very wet. The instant Clint's fingers touched the tender lips, Gwen grabbed his shoulders and shuddered. Clint looked over to Allie and found her standing nearby, watching. Her naked body looked creamy in the pale light spilling in from outside and her stockings made the texture of her skin seem even more attractive. Allie's hands wandered over her own body and her breasts heaved with her quickening breath.

Clint moved his hands over to Allie so he could guide her down to the floor. He lowered himself onto his back and she settled right on top of him. Allie straddled his hips until Clint could feel her stockings brushing against the outside of his legs. She was slow to lower herself any farther, but was unable to hold back for long once she felt Clint's rock-hard erection graze against her vagina.

For a few seconds, Allie simply rubbed herself against his cock, savoring the way it felt on her. Clint put one hand on her hip and used the other to guide himself inside. Once he'd penetrated her, Allie dropped all the way down to envelop him completely.

"Oh, God," Allie moaned. "Oh—" Her next words were taken away as Clint grabbed both hips and began pumping up into her. She quickly adjusted to his rhythm and placed her hands flat upon his stomach so she could grind her hips every time he impaled her.

Clint looked up to find Gwen watching with wide eyes. He lifted one hand and motioned for her to come closer and she was more than willing to oblige.

Gwen knelt down and ran her hands along Clint's chest. She was still wearing her dress, although the upper portion was bunched around her waist. That way, Clint could pull on her skirts to guide her toward where he wanted her to be. She caught on quickly and hiked up her skirts so she could reposition herself accordingly.

Straddling his head, Gwen held her skirts up and looked down as Clint lifted his mouth to her dripping pussy. He flickered his tongue quickly over her pink lips, which caused Gwen to reach down and grab a handful of his hair.

"Good Lord," Gwen moaned. "You are full of surprises."

Clint couldn't see Allie any longer, but he could still feel her riding his cock. When he looked up, his eyes got a healthy dose of Gwen's pendulous breasts swinging freely above him. She squatted down even lower so he could truly bury his face between her legs. Clint slipped his tongue

inside of her and moved it in and out at the same pace as
Allie bouncing up and down on top of him.

After a few minutes, Gwen tightened her grip on Clint's
hair. He flicked his tongue even faster until he could hear her
crying out as she climaxed. Although he was a little afraid
she might rip out the hair she was holding, Gwen loosened
her grip as her orgasm passed through her. She then stood up
and stepped aside so Clint could once more see Allie.

Eyes clenched shut and her face twisted with the effort
of grinding on top of him, Allie moaned steadily as her pussy
tightened around Clint's cock. Now he could see that Allie
had been the one holding Gwen's skirts out of the way.
Allie still held on to them as if she were gripping the reins
of a bucking horse.

Clint rolled Allie onto her back and got on top of her.
She wrapped her legs around him, but didn't seem to have
the strength to keep her head up. Instead, Allie closed her
eyes and moaned breathlessly as Clint thrust his hips between her legs. It didn't take long for him to push her over
the edge and Allie writhed against the floor as her own climax worked its way through her.

Pumping into her one last time, Clint caused Allie to let
out one more groan that echoed within the otherwise silent
shop. He then stood up and set his sights on Gwen. "Turn
around," he told her.

Gwen's eyes lit up and she did as she was told.

Clint stepped behind her, pulled her skirts up, and positioned her so Gwen was facing a stack of anvils piled in
one corner. The moment he placed his hand upon her lower
back, Clint felt her lean forward and stretch her backside
toward him. He rubbed Gwen's ample hips and then entered her from behind.

Gwen grabbed the anvils in front of her and braced herself as Clint began pumping into her again and again. She

grunted and groaned while occasionally looking back at him to show the wicked smile that had overtaken her face.

After driving all the way into her, Clint reached around to cup Gwen's breasts. She straightened up so he could move his hands freely over the front of her naked body and she spread her legs a little farther apart so Clint could move a little easier between them.

Soon, Clint felt Allie's bare breasts graze against his back as she came up behind him. She reached around to let her hands wander up and down over the muscles of his chest and down to his abdomen. As Clint thrust in and out of Gwen, Allie rubbed against his thigh and waited for her next turn.

NINETEEN

The next morning, it seemed as if the entire town was suffering from the festivities of the night before. The air wasn't just quiet. It was absolutely still. When a breeze did manage to wind through the streets, it only managed to blow around some tattered banners or other trash that hadn't been picked up. Shutters creaked and a few dogs barked, but there weren't many clues that Red Water wasn't just a recently abandoned ghost town.

When the line of horses left the stable and marched down Sales Street, the crunch of hooves against dirt echoed like gunshots down the empty avenues. There were nine men in all. Marshal Flynt led the group, with one of his deputies on either side. Behind the lawmen, Clint and Arvin rode with another posse member who had been playing the banjo during the previous night's dancing. The remaining men had all been at Dale's, but a vast majority of the group who'd heard Flynt's speech hadn't bothered leaving the comfort of the saloon.

The deputy to Flynt's left was the tall redhead who'd dragged Clint into the alley. He looked even more imposing on the back of a horse and he didn't try to hide the distaste he felt when he turned around to catch sight of Clint. "Is this all we could find?" he asked.

Flynt didn't bother looking behind him. "This'll be plenty," he said with a casual wave over his shoulder. "I'm surprised we got this many to join up at all."

"Weren't there more that signed the book?"

"Sure there was, but they ain't here now." Flynt finally did turn around to get a look at the men behind him. "More reward for us!"

Despite the fact that his comment only got a few half-hearted nods from the posse, Flynt settled into his saddle as if he were at the head of an adoring army of followers.

Clint merely shook his head and kept his chuckle to himself as much as he could. "Where are we headed?" he asked.

"Out of town and to the northwest," Flynt replied.

"I could have figured out that much on my own. I meant where are we headed once we leave Red Water? Do you know where those outlaws are?"

"You said they attacked you," the redheaded deputy growled. "Maybe you should ride on ahead and see if they can chase you around some more."

"That'll be enough of that kind of talk, Tom," Flynt scolded. "All these men have signed on to help, so I won't let you fight among yourselves."

"Good," Clint said. "Perhaps I can turn my back on him without worrying he might try to bushwhack me."

"Bushwhack, like hell!" Tom snapped.

"That," Flynt said quickly, "was a misunderstanding. We're all on the same page now, so let's act like it and get this job done."

Tom glared at Clint with a look in his eyes that would have withered most healthy oak trees. Clint stared right back at him, without bothering to stare the redhead down. Instead,

Clint kept one hand wrapped loosely around Eclipse's reins and the other resting within easy reach of his holster.

"Why the hell are we riding with him?" Tom asked.

"Because there ain't no reason not to," Flynt replied. "If anyone else has a problem with Clint Adams, tell it to me right now!"

If anything, the rest of the posse merely looked interested in the possibility of seeing Tom and Clint throw punches right then and there. When Marshal Flynt looked at them each in turn, the locals shrugged their shoulders or shook their heads.

"Good," Flynt said proudly. "That's settled. Now, Clint. You were the last one to lay eyes on these killers. Do you know which way they went?"

"I was camped east of town," Clint explained. "I led them away from there to the north and circled back around until I left them in the dust. After that, I didn't have any cause to follow them. I suppose I could take you back to the camp and I can pick up their tracks from there."

"You ain't the only tracker in this outfit," Tom said.

"Fine," Clint replied. "I'll just follow your lead as you wander around looking at every last dent or shoeprint left behind by any number of horses ridden by any number of—"

"Fine, fine," Flynt cut in. "Clint's camp is as good a place to start as any."

Pulling back on his reins, Clint stopped just short of Red Water's northernmost limit. "Just head east and I'll catch up to you men shortly."

"What are you doing?" Tom asked.

"Just playing a hunch before I take you to my campsite. It won't take long to see it through and it may pay off sooner than you think."

"What hunch, goddamn it?"

"I could explain myself and waste more time or I can see it through and meet up with you before you're a mile outside of town. Either one doesn't make much difference to me."

"Just let him go, Tom," Flynt barked. Shifting his eyes to Clint, he added, "And you . . . whatever you're doing be quick about it. If we don't see you inside half an hour, you'd best keep riding and pray we don't cross paths again."

"You run off with your tail between your legs and you'll see me again!" Tom added. "And it won't be friendly like the last time we met."

Clint rode away without looking back. More than anything, he wanted to laugh in Marshal Flynt's face and punch Tom in his. Since he didn't think he could act concerned enough to make either of the lawmen satisfied, he just threw a quick wave over his shoulder.

The only thing that made him want to come back to that posse at all was the fact that Flynt and his men were acting even more suspicious now than they had before. They were definitely up to something and Clint truly wanted to be the one to bring that plan to light and crack it wide open.

TWENTY

Clint had come up with his idea sometime after last night's supper. Unfortunately, he'd been too busy dancing to do anything about it that night and he'd had his hands full all the way until early morning to do anything then. He'd truly almost completely forgotten about it until he was on his way out of town.

It was a short ride back to Tanner Hall and he jumped down from the saddle before Eclipse even came to a stop. Snapping the reins around a hitching post, Clint bolted inside to have a talk with some of the workers in the place. A few minutes later, Clint made the rounds to a few more spots in town and then hopped onto Eclipse's back one more time.

Clint figured he could still catch up to the posse with plenty of time to spare and fought back the urge to get a cup of coffee somewhere before subjecting himself to the company of Marshal Flynt and his gang of assholes. The only thing that allowed him to do that was the thought of how sweet it would be to throw whatever those lawmen were doing right back in their faces.

If Clint had ever had any doubt that something fishy was going on, it would have been wiped away by seeing the lawmen that morning. From the moment Flynt and Tom had met up with the rest of the posse, they'd been chomping at the bit to get out of town, even when it was clear they didn't have a solid plan to go after those outlaws.

No lawman formed a posse unless he already had somewhere for them to go. The whole reason for a posse was to collect able-bodied souls who could lend numbers to go against armed fugitives. If Flynt didn't know where to find Laramie and his gang, he had no need of more men.

If there was some other pressing need to assemble a posse, Clint would have seen it just by keeping his eyes and ears open. Nothing had happened in town the last few days and the rowdy Founder's Day celebration would have been the perfect time for more trouble to be stirred up. As far as Clint could tell, the only thing that happened during Founder's Day was that the women of Red Water got hot under the collar.

There was no law against that.

The only thing that bothered Clint more than Flynt's peculiar behavior was the fact that he couldn't put his finger on the reason for it. If the lawman were just up to shady business, Clint might have just left him to it. But Flynt was gathering armed men and putting them to use under the color of authority. It wouldn't take a brilliant tactician to cause some trouble with a posse at his command.

Something was rotten in Red Water, something that had to do with the marshal, the posse, or the deputies—but that didn't narrow it down much at all. More than anything, uncertainty nagged at Clint like an itch he couldn't quite scratch.

That itch caused him to finish up his rounds and get

Eclipse racing out of town once again. And it was that itch that made him point his nose in the direction the posse was headed rather than some other direction that led to simpler, quieter places.

TWENTY-ONE

Despite all of the marshal's demands that Clint hurry up, Flynt obviously didn't intend on leaving Clint behind. Eclipse may have been running at a faster pace than most other horses could manage, but Clint still caught up with the posse in half the time he'd guessed it would take. When he rode up to the group, it was just as easy for Clint to see the relief on Flynt's face as it was to spot the disappointment on Tom's.

"You get your business squared away?" the marshal asked.

Clint nodded. "Just like I promised."

"Good. Now you can uphold the promise you made to me. Where's that camp of yours?"

"Just keep heading east. Once we get a little closer, I should be able to lead us the rest of the way in."

"Should?" Tom growled. "What's that supposed to mean? You either can or you can't."

"It was just a spot I picked on a whim," Clint told the deputy. "I made a fire, had something to drink, and slept for a bit. I wasn't about to mark the place on a map."

Tom rolled his eyes and groaned, "For Christ's sake."

"Anyone else got a better idea?" Flynt asked.

The posse members all looked as if they'd suddenly been asked to put together a plan for managing a small country. Their eyes glazed over and they shook their heads.

"I say we should head to all the other towns within a day's ride and ask around if anyone's seen Laramie or heard-tell of where he might be," Tom offered.

Flynt nodded. "All right. How far away is this camp of yours, Adams?"

"If we start riding and stop dawdling, we should be able to get there well before nightfall."

"Since that'll take a lot less time than scattering and striking out for towns that are a hell of a lot farther, we'll head for Clint's camp." Fixing his eyes upon Tom to cut off the deputy before he could complain, the marshal added, "And if we don't find the camp or if there ain't nothing to see once we get there, we'll switch to the other plan."

"If them killers ain't already skinned out by then," Tom grumbled.

Unable to take any more guff from the redhead, Clint said, "And I suppose riding off to some random other town will be better! Why don't we all just spread out, ride across the entire county, and call out the names of the men we're after? There's just as big a chance of getting lucky with that plan as there is in roaming aimlessly from one town to another."

Tom didn't have an answer to that, but he sure looked like he had something else for Clint. One of the redhead's fists was balled up tightly and the other twitched toward the gun at his side.

"Go on and skin that gun of yours," Clint said. "See how far you get before I knock you on your ass."

"Enough!" Flynt barked.

Tom was still perched on the edge of his saddle and

Arvin was more than ready to back the deputy's play. Clint could feel the bad intentions coming from Arvin like heat being given off by a rock that had spent an entire summer in the desert sun.

Circling his horse around to cut Tom off, Flynt positioned himself so the entire, slow-moving group had to come to a halt. The marshal's hand slapped against the grip of his .45 as he snarled, "I don't want to draw on either one of you men and I sure as hell don't want to waste another second bickering like a bunch of children!

"You see this badge?" Flynt asked as he tapped his finger against the tin hanging from the front of his shirt. "This means I'm in charge of this outfit and I say we check out the camp. If it turns out to be nothing, I'll deal with it! Understand me?"

"Sure do, Marshal," Clint replied amiably.

"Tom?"

The redhead nodded just enough for the gesture to be seen. He had yet to take his eyes off Clint.

"Good. I won't say another word on this again," Flynt declared. "If either of you men become more trouble than you're worth, I'll drop you like a bad habit."

For some reason, that seemed to get under Tom's skin. Since Clint was still looking straight into the redhead's eyes, he could see the subtle flinch that tipped the deputy's hand. Tom might have sensed that as well, because he nodded and looked away.

Knowing a victory when he saw it, Flynt wasn't about to press for anything more. "Fine," he said. "Clint, lead the way."

The pained scowl on Tom's face was replaced by a sly grin. The expression came and went like a flicker, but that was more than enough to catch Clint's attention.

"Just like I said before, Marshal," Clint replied. "Keep

heading east and I'll let you know when we need to change direction. I'm more than willing for you to take your spot at the front."

Tom obviously liked the notion of having Clint's back in his sights, but if he wanted that to happen he would need to speak up. Apparently, the deputy wasn't prepared to be so bold. And, just as Clint had suspected, Flynt was plenty happy to puff out his chest and lead the charge.

"That's respect, Tom," Flynt pointed out. "Perhaps it's good Adams stays with us. You could learn a thing or two from him." He then snapped his reins and the rest of the posse was quick to follow.

Clint rode with the others, but made certain all of them were in plain view. They rode for several miles with Tom quietly steaming over the marshal's last comment. It was all Clint could do to keep from chuckling at it all. He couldn't have gotten under Tom's skin worse if he'd tried.

TWENTY-TWO

It took a good, long while for Clint to find the spot of his old camp. Despite all of Tom's grousing, the slow progress wasn't due to any effort on Clint's part to muck them up. Clint had been more than honest in what he'd told the marshal. The last time he'd been at the camp, Clint's main concern was counting the holes in his eyelids. Trying to find that same spot again was akin to finding where he'd been standing the previous week when a particular butterfly had fluttered past his nose.

And yet, even with Tom's grousing, Clint managed to find the camp.

Just when Clint had thought the search was a lost cause, a couple stands of trees caught his eye. He got that nagging sensation of recall as if he had spotted a vaguely familiar face in a crowd. He rode a little closer until something else struck his fancy. A few minutes after that, he reined Eclipse to a stop and climbed down from the saddle.

"Is this the spot?" Flynt asked.

Before Clint could respond, Tom growled, "It damn well better be."

"Or what, Tom?" Clint asked. He hadn't meant to do anything to draw any more attention to himself, but the question had come out before Clint could stop it. After riding this far with the deputy, he finally had enough of the redhead's whining.

Tom smirked and shook his head. Somewhere during the ride, he'd reined himself in enough to get his point across while also staying in the marshal's good graces.

Resisting the urge to goad the deputy any further, Clint walked past a few of the trees until he found the spot he'd been after. "This is the place," he announced. "I was sitting right here when I heard those horse thieves come around."

"And you're sure it was Laramie?" Flynt asked.

"There were three of them. One was a black fellow, who didn't say much of anything. Another was a young kid called Harvey. He's the one that looks like the man named Laramie on your reward notice. The third looked like the other man on the notice."

"Chris Jerrison?" Flynt asked hopefully.

Nodding, Clint said, "I don't know about the last name, but he was called Chris."

"And how'd you hear all this?" Arvin asked. "You said you was chasing them around or they was chasing you."

Still biting his tongue, Tom looked at Arvin and nodded approvingly.

"I was able to circle around and listen to them talk for a bit," Clint said.

Flynt hopped down from his saddle and stomped over to stand beside Clint. Along the way, he impatiently waved at the rest of his men. "I already heard the story and it sounds like the men we're after. Now let's see if we can find any tracks."

From there, Flynt hunkered down and studied the dirt as if he were squinting at the small print in a smudged newspaper.

He was concentrating so intensely that everyone else in the area reflexively quieted down so as not to disturb him.

A few seconds ticked by and the only sounds to be heard were the rustling of the leaves and the breath of the horses. Before too long, Flynt looked up and asked, "Well, ain't you going to look for tracks?"

Clint felt as if he'd been rudely awakened from a deep sleep. Then, once he realized the marshal's tracking was a half-assed charade, he had to cover his laugh by clearing his throat. "Oh, sure. Let me just take a look here."

Starting at the tree where he recalled sitting and looking up at the stars, Clint looked around for traces he'd left behind. When he found them, he at least knew he was in the right spot. He then widened his search by moving off in the direction he'd gone when he'd circled to get around and behind the horse thieves. The lawmen stood back to watch Clint, and the other posse members were content to relax and swap a few jokes amongst themselves.

Clint did his best to recall what the horse thieves had done and in which direction they'd ridden so he could get a handle on where to look for tracks. It had been more than a day, but the ground was mostly flat and covered by trampled grass, which made it slightly easier to spot imprints. Looking up at the waiting lawmen, Clint said, "I found them."

Flynt's eyes widened and he rushed over to Clint's side. "You did? Show me."

"You don't believe me?"

"It'd do best if more than one of us knows what tracks we're following."

"You're a tracker, then?"

The marshal blinked, ground his teeth together, and admitted, "No, but I can pick it up easy enough."

"I can follow tracks pretty good," Frank volunteered.

Since those were the first words he'd said all day, everyone in the posse turned to make sure their ears weren't playing tricks on them. Noticing all the eyes fixed upon him, Frank added, "I ain't no trailsman, but I used to hunt bounties before I signed on as a deputy."

"Why didn't you tell me you was a tracker?" Flynt asked.

"I ain't a tracker. I got good eyes, is all. If he points the tracks out to me, I should be able to pick 'em out well enough to follow 'em."

Clint stood up and pointed down to the spot he'd been studying. "You see that?" he asked.

Frank leaned forward in his saddle and squinted. "What?"

"Those shoe prints in the dirt. The way the grass is torn up. The ground that's been kicked up."

"Yeah, I see that."

"Which way do they lead?"

After a bit of consideration, Frank said, "East. No, that's where they come from. Looks like they're headed north. I think that's another set behind you. That one looks to head west . . . more or less."

Clint nodded. "He's right. They scattered and then came back around to me."

"Perfect," Flynt said with a beaming smile. "We'll split up and follow both sets of tracks. Since the gang isn't known for splitting up, the tracks should lead us to all meet up again soon enough."

TWENTY-THREE

Frank actually wasn't a bad tracker. As much as he disliked the deputy for that scuffle in the alley, Clint had to admit as much just by watching the man lead the others around in circles in the distance. As near as Clint could remember, those were awfully close to the same circles the thieves had made when they were trying to regain control of their spooked horses.

Clint had a couple of the locals accompanying him as he followed the other set of tracks. Only one man opened his mouth for more than a yawn and he seemed like a good enough fellow. His name was Baker and Clint had to assume that was his last name, since no other had been given. Baker looked to be the runt of the litter, but he sat in his saddle as if he'd been born on a horse's back. The holster around his waist was well weathered and the gun looked to be properly cared for.

"You ride along with a posse before, Baker?" Clint asked.

"Maybe a few. Why?"

"Because you look more suited for this than some of those lawmen."

Baker winced and looked over his shoulder as if the marshal and his men could hear Clint despite all the distance between them. "Marshal Flynt means well enough."

"I'm sure he does. It just seems that they don't really have much of a plan out here."

One of the other posse members chimed in. "We're supposed to get paid whether they find those men or not. You ain't heard any different, have you?"

Clint looked over at a slouching man in his thirties with a face covered by uneven stubble and a curtain of stringy, greasy hair. Until now, Clint wasn't even sure what the man's voice sounded like.

"I haven't heard any different," Clint assured him, "but I just think it's peculiar that—"

"Just so long as we get paid," the greasy man interrupted. "Suits me just fine if'n we don't find them outlaws."

Baker shook his head as if to apologize for the greasy man's apathy. Clint leaned toward him and asked, "What exactly were you men told?"

"That this was an easy paycheck," Baker replied. "When we went up to so much as look at that book we signed, Marshal Flynt said we'd get a handsome fee no matter what."

"You don't seem too anxious to get that reward."

"Fact of the matter is that the marshal made it sound like we probably wouldn't find the men anyhow. The fee's enough to make it worth our while to take a few days and ride around for a bit, though."

Clint nodded and took it all in. One thing that struck him now was that Baker seemed to be one of the only normal men he'd spoken to in this affair. Just to check that theory, Clint asked, "Doesn't any of this seem strange to you?"

Reluctantly, Baker nodded. "Yeah, but I wasn't gonna say anything. I could use the money. We all could."

"Never look a gift horse in the mouth!" the greasy man said. "Remember that and we'll all be home with full pockets."

Although Baker wasn't about to argue with that, he shifted in his saddle for a few seconds before asking, "You think something else is goin' on here?"

Clint pulled back on his reins, bringing all the men to a stop. "Take a look over there," he said while pointing to the lawmen in the distance. "They've been milling around there all this time."

"Frank said he wasn't a tracker," Baker pointed out. "He's just got good eyes."

"Sure, but they would have either found tracks by now or come back to let us know they haven't found anything. For a bunch of men out to hunt down such vicious killers, they don't seem to be in much of a hurry."

"They're the ones with the gift horse, Adams!" the greasy man pointed out. "Don't look it in the damned mouth."

"Shut the hell up, Lefty," Baker snapped.

Lefty grunted and swiped his hand at Baker while steering his horse in another direction.

Clint didn't care what Lefty did, since Baker had proven to be a whole lot more useful. Even though he figured Lefty wasn't listening, Clint lowered his voice to make sure what he said next was strictly between him and Baker. "I've just spotted those tracks again, but they head back toward town."

"Really?" Baker asked.

Clint nodded. "Do you want to find out if Flynt and those deputies are any more interested in catching outlaws than your friend Lefty over there?"

Baker raised an eyebrow and leaned over to whisper, "We stand to make a lot more with the reward than the scraps that fat lawman's willing to toss at us."

"I like the way you think."

TWENTY-FOUR

Clint, Baker, and Lefty rode back to join the rest of the posse. When they got there, they found Marshal Flynt and his deputies milling about as if they were enjoying the weather. "I found them!" Clint declared.

Flynt looked a little surprised, but none of the others seemed very impressed.

"What did you find?" Tom asked. "More tracks?"

"That's what we were looking for, wasn't it?" Clint replied. "What have you men been doing all this time?"

"For your information," Flynt said, "we found tracks of our own. They lead to the north and they look like they were put down in a rush. Ain't that right, Frank?"

"Yeah," Frank replied. "Pretty fresh, too."

Clint nodded slowly. "I would have thought those men were long gone from here, but they must have come back if the tracks are fresh like you say they are."

"What about the tracks you found?" Flynt asked. "Do they hook up toward the north as well?"

"Nope. They lead to the west."

"I saw them, too," Baker added. "Looks like they head back toward Red Water."

Flynt looked at each of his deputies in turn, but his eyes settled upon the redhead. "Why don't you go along with them, Tom? See where those tracks really lead."

Tom nodded and moved his horse to stand alongside Clint.

"No need to break up the groups," Clint told him. "Since you men know what you're looking for and we've seen our own tracks, we can just follow them and meet up back in town. If one of us comes up empty, we shouldn't have any trouble catching up to the other."

Flynt shook his head insistently. "No. Tom should go with you. He's got the law behind him in case you do run into those outlaws."

"We've all got the law behind us, Marshal. That's why you deputized us."

The marshal chewed on that, but didn't seem to like the taste of it. "Tom's going with you. If you don't like it, you can come along with us and he'll follow those tracks alone."

Smiling good-naturedly, Clint said, "I don't have any problem with that. Just trying to make things easier, is all. What's the plan from here, Marshal?"

"There's a town north of here called Springston," Flynt said. "By the looks of it, that's where Laramie's headed. I hear-tell that he's even got some family up that way."

"Yeah," Lefty grunted. "I think I heard something about that."

"You see?" Flynt declared happily. "Those outlaws are probably holed up somewhere near Springston where they can get rested up and lay low with some family to protect them. Those other tracks are probably just them trying to throw us off their tails."

"Or they were put down when Adams was running around trying to lose them before," Tom pointed out.

Flynt chuckled and then coughed to cover it up. "That

ain't polite, Tom. But, to be fair, he did mention before that he rode about to turn them around."

"Yeah," Clint said dryly. "I mentioned something like that."

"Then Tom'll go with you to see how far them tracks go before they hook up north again. You might just find one of them fellas on their own somewhere. Perhaps that black one from the notice skinned out to Kyle's Ridge. That's less than a day's ride southwest of Red Water."

Biting his tongue before saying another word, Clint simply nodded again.

"There you go," Flynt said. "We're all in agreement. Clint and Tom will go see how far those other tracks go and then we can meet up again in Springston. If Laramie ain't there, we'll head down to Kyle's Ridge and if they ain't there, then they're probably in Canada or Old Mexico."

All the deputies nodded as if their heads were attached to springs and most of the posse members looked like they couldn't care less.

"I'll go along with Clint," Baker offered.

Flynt was already turning away and had to shift back around again to look at who'd spoken. Apparently, this was one of the first times he'd heard Baker speak. "What? Why?"

"I said I'll go with Clint. I spotted those tracks, too, so if he loses sight of them, I can—"

"We don't need you," Tom growled. "Just do what the marshal says."

"No, Tom," Flynt told him. "It's all right. You three go. Just be quick about it." With that, the marshal and the remaining men got moving toward the north.

"Come on," Tom said. "Let's get this over with."

TWENTY-FIVE

Not a word was said during the short ride back to the spot where Clint and Baker had had their previous conversation. Once they were there, both men pulled back on their reins and waited for Tom to catch up. The deputy had been content to ride a few paces behind and stopped so as to keep the same distance between them.

Clint swung down from his saddle and started examining the ground. "We spotted those tracks right around here," he said.

"If they were this close to Red Water, they could be anything, you know," Tom pointed out. "There's men riding into town all the time, not to mention wagons and stagecoaches that roll through on their way to damn near anywhere else."

"The same could be said about the tracks you found," Clint said.

Baker added his own two cents with, "You never even showed us them tracks the marshal was talking about."

Tom shifted his eyes to the posse member as if he were sighting along the top of a rifle. "What the hell's that supposed to mean? You callin' me and the marshal liars?"

"No. I just said we never got to look at those other

tracks. Maybe we could'a helped follow them. Ain't that why we're all out here?"

"No. You're here to—"

"Good," Clint interrupted. "I'd like to hear this. Tell us why we're all out here."

Freezing with his mouth still wrapped around the words he'd meant to say, Tom narrowed his eyes and looked back and forth between the two men in front of him. "You know why we're here. It's to catch them outlaws, not follow every rut you find in the ground."

"Why are you so dead set against going back to Red Water?" The moment he asked that question, Clint could tell he'd hit a nerve. Taking a step forward to press the issue even further, he said, "Those outlaws could have gone there. Marshal Flynt was spouting off about that very possibility when he was gathering up all these locals, but now he wants to go anywhere but back to Red Water. Why is that, Tom?"

The deputy spoke in a low growl that was barely enough to get his lips moving. "We don't have to explain ourselves to you or anybody. You do what the marshal tells you to do or you shouldn't have signed up for this posse. Since you have signed up, do what you're fucking told."

"We were promised a shot at that reward," Baker said. "If we aren't gonna get that, we deserve—"

"You don't deserve shit!" Tom barked as he drew his pistol from its holster. Pointing the weapon at Baker, he placed his thumb on the hammer and his finger against the trigger. "If you intend on questioning every goddamn move, I'm of a mind to think you're in league with those outlaws!"

Baker's mouth hung open and the color drained from his face. Although Tom seemed to like that reaction, he didn't like what came next.

Clint grabbed hold of the deputy's free arm and yanked

Tom from the saddle so his legs were plucked from the stir-
rups and his gun whipped toward the sky. The pistol's trigger guard snagged on Tom's finger, but wasn't fired before
its owner hit the ground.

Tom slammed against the earth in a heap. His horse
started to fret at all the sudden activity, but didn't do more
than huff and fidget from one leg to another. Before he
could fill his lungs again, Tom found himself looking up at
Clint's face.

"I don't know what pisses me off more," Clint said as he
grappled with Tom's gun hand. "The way you figured I'd
bow down and forget you tried to break my neck in that alley or the fact that Marshal Flynt obviously takes me and
the rest of this posse for raving fools."

After hitting the ground on his side, Tom strained to
right himself while also fighting to keep hold of his gun.
Once he had his legs beneath him, he got up and pulled in
his .44 with all the strength he had. Clint wasn't about to let
go, which was just fine by the deputy, who snapped his
head forward to drive his forehead into Clint's nose.

There was a jarring impact, mixed with a wet crunch
that filled Clint's entire head. He was dazed and nearly
gave in to the fog that filled his brain, but he still managed
to keep his grip on Tom's weapon. Suddenly, the .44 came
away from Tom's grasp, leaving Clint with his hands
wrapped around the barrel and cylinder. The moment he
tried to shift to a proper hold on the pistol, it was slapped
completely away from him.

Tom then reached for another gun he'd stashed in a rig
strapped to his shoulder. He had just managed to touch the
handle of the .38 when Clint rushed him like a bull.

Clint's shoulder slammed against the taut muscle of
Tom's midsection. Although he didn't knock the deputy off
his feet, Clint did manage to stagger him back a ways.

Tom's arms dropped onto Clint's back and shoulders like clubs, slowly turning the tide of the fight in his favor.

Suddenly, there was another impact that Clint could feel through his whole body. This time, however, he didn't catch the brunt of the impact. Clint could feel it because Tom had been hit hard enough for some of the force to make it all the way through him like ripples on the surface of a pond.

Twisting around toward the source of the impact, Tom spotted Baker and bared his teeth at the posse member as if he fully intended to tear his throat out. Ignoring the effects of the last few hits he'd taken, Tom grabbed hold of Baker's shirt in one hand and continued to draw his .38 with the other.

"That's the last mistake you'll make," Tom swore.

Just as Tom's .38 cleared leather, Clint's modified Colt cracked against the side of the deputy's head.

Tom's head snapped to one side and he stumbled in that direction. It took a few more steps, however, for him to drop to one knee. Once he did, Clint was right there to grab the .38 from Tom's hand.

"You'll . . . hang for this," Tom groaned. "Both of you."

TWENTY-SIX

"I've got to admit," Clint said as he pushed the deputy to the ground and held him there with his boot, "you really impressed me. That's a real hard head you got there."

"What you done . . . it's . . . you'll hang for it."

"I know, I know. Normally, I don't much approve of knocking a lawman around like that, but you were about to shoot a member of your own posse for no good reason. From where I stand, that doesn't make you much of a lawman."

Tom sucked in a few breaths that Clint could feel through the sole of his boot. Before the deputy could gather any more strength, Clint leaned more of his weight down and placed his elbow on his knee. "It's just us out here now, Tom," he said. "There's no reason to keep lying and there's nobody around to back you up. Despite that hard head of yours, you couldn't even take me when you had partners back in that alley."

That one stuck in Tom's craw. When he squirmed under Clint's boot, there was a little more strength than there had been before. Clint turned and slowly placed his hand upon the grip of his holstered Colt. Despite everything that had come before, he still didn't like the idea of pulling a gun on a deputy. Fortunately, his bluff wasn't about to be called.

The moment Clint's hand settled upon the Colt, Tom stopped moving.

"Tell me what's really going on here," Clint demanded.

"Or what?" Tom grunted. "You'll kill me? You can't even draw your gun."

"I don't draw my gun unless I'm about to pull the trigger. When I draw this gun, it'll be too late for you to say a damn thing to stop me."

Baker stepped in close enough for Clint to see him without taking his eyes off Tom. Despite the fact that Clint could only see the posse member's legs, he could tell Baker was rattled.

"There's no reason for anyone to get shot here," Baker said in a trembling voice. "We just want to know why we were all brought out here."

"Step aside," Clint said. "This is between me and Tom."

Clint didn't want to threaten Baker, but it was the only way to maintain the tone he'd set for the conversation while also discouraging Baker from calling his bluff. Unfortunately, Baker wasn't about to be pushed aside so easily.

"I agree that something ain't right," Baker said. "Marshal Flynt put together the best posse anyone could, but all he's doin' with them is runnin' them from one spot to another."

At that moment, the thing that had been nagging at the back of Clint's mind started nagging even more. It was like a tick burrowing under his skin until it stumbled upon a soft spot. "What did you say?" he asked.

Baker had settled down a bit now that he seemed to have drawn Clint's eye away from Tom. "I said I agree that—"

"No, I meant about Marshal Flynt putting the posse together."

It took a moment for Baker to sift through his racing thoughts, but he found what he was after soon enough. "Oh, I said he got the best posse he could expect. Considering the folks in Red Water, he got damn near all the most capable men to sign on one way or another. The ones that passed on the job were either too old or too wide around the middle to do any good out here."

Clint looked back at Tom, just as the redhead was easing his hands toward the boot planted upon his chest. Glaring down at the deputy as if he could see straight through to the ground beneath Tom's head, Clint was able to make the deputy think twice about trying to grab the offending boot. "That was the idea, wasn't it?" Clint asked.

Tom gritted his teeth and stared defiantly up at Clint in a way that somehow made it seem he was looking down on him. "What nonsense are you spitting out now?"

"Something's happening in Red Water." Although Tom didn't say anything to confirm that, Clint didn't need him to. "The posse wasn't intended to go after those outlaws or anyone else. It was intended to get all the capable gunhands out of town."

"That's a pile of horseshit," Tom scoffed.

Clint shook his head slowly. "I don't think so. Marshal Flynt may not be as sharp as they come, but he can't be as incompetent as he's making himself out to be. Somewhere along the line, even one of you deputies would have stopped to ask a few questions here and there. But you haven't, have you?"

"It ain't our place to question orders."

Baker stepped closer, but didn't seem so intent now on getting between Clint and Tom. The expression on his face had turned around completely to reflect eagerness rather than panic. "I heard you were a military man, Tom."

"So?"

"You don't do anything without a plan. You say as much every time you bring in a drunk or break up a fight at a saloon. You're smarter than just some idiot who forms a posse to run in circles. Hell," Baker added, "even Marshal Flynt is smarter than that."

Whether Baker had ruffled the deputy's feathers or had hit too close to the mark, Tom started to sit up and raise his hands as if he intended on throttling the posse member right then and there. Fortunately for Baker, Clint's boot was still in place and he was able to force the redhead down once more.

"What's going on in Red Water?" Clint asked. "You might as well tell us."

"There's gonna be a trial," Tom snapped. "That's what's gonna happen in Red Water. Or maybe there'll be a hanging. Either way, you two ain't about to walk away after attacking a duly appointed man of the law."

Clint couldn't help but smirk. "Those are some fancy words for a man that doesn't even know what to do with a posse. You truly think you'll still be duly appointed when it comes out that you had a part in this business?"

"Nobody will know a damn thing!"

"Is that so?" Clint asked. "A damn thing about what?"

Tom shut his mouth so quickly that he nearly bit off the end of his tongue. The corners of both eyes were twitching and the muscles were tensing beneath Clint's boot. Before the deputy could make the move he was thinking about, Clint held up the hand that was gripping Tom's .38.

"Go on and shoot, Adams," Tom snarled. "That'll only bring the others here quicker. They're probably on their way already."

"Tell me what's going on in town," Clint said. "It's over one way or another, so you might as well come clean."

"Why should I? You think I believe you'll just turn me loose as a show of good faith?"

"No, but I'll come after you last. If you're the smart military man Baker thinks you are, then you stand a chance of getting away. Or you could even come back around to try your gun against mine. Either one would be fine with me."

There was a glimmer in Tom's eye when he heard the second choice. Still, his mouth remained shut tighter than a sprung trap.

"Fine," Clint said after a few seconds. "We'll just go and do some digging on our own."

"What are we . . . I mean . . . what do we do with him?" Baker stammered.

"Simple," Clint replied. "We just make sure nobody's able to find him and they'll figure we all rode off to Springston. That was the plan, right, Tom?"

That was the first time Clint saw even a hint of fear in the deputy's eyes.

TWENTY-SEVEN

Tom put up a hell of a fight when Clint tried to do more than hold him down with his boot. The moment Clint asked Baker for a rope, Tom knew he had to fight for his freedom. The struggle was as quick as it was furious. Tom grabbed hold of Clint's boot and tried to twist his foot off, but Clint was able to shift his weight and drop his elbow onto the deputy's midsection.

Tom's breath came out in a single gust, doubling him over like a caterpillar curling up on itself. Clint tried to get ahold of Tom's arms, but the deputy was too strong to be subdued just yet. After that, the two men wrestled amid a flurry of fists, elbows, knees, and damn near anything else they could throw at one another.

When Baker tried to get the rope to Clint, he caught a wild punch in the face and didn't even know who'd thrown it. After taking that punch, Baker dove into the fight and was able to pull Tom off Clint for about a second or two. That was just enough time for Clint to land one solid punch on Tom's jaw that knocked the deputy out cold.

"Damn," Clint said as he shook his aching fist. "Good thing he was too proud to call for help."

Judging by the look on Baker's face, it was only just occurring to him what had happened. "He's right," he gasped. "We'll hang for this. You can't just knock out a deputy and get away with it."

"Help me get him tied up and then we can discuss the rest."

Baker was rattled, but he went along with Clint's request. Between the two of them, they got Tom's arms tied behind his back, his legs trussed up, and a few bandannas wrapped over his mouth. Just to be on the safe side, Clint looped the rest of his rope around the big deputy and tied it all together with a triple knot.

"What now?" Baker asked as he looked at the unconscious deputy.

Clint wiped his brow and looked in the direction he'd last seen the rest of the lawmen. "Now we need to put this one where he won't be found."

"Oh, Lord. You don't mean burying him do you?"

"Settle down, Baker. If I'm right about any of this, the marshal and his men are up to something rotten and they won't be wearing badges when it's over. Even so, I'm not about to kill someone just to keep his mouth shut."

Baker let out a slow breath and nodded. Still, his relief didn't last long. "And what if you're wrong?" he asked meekly.

"If I'm wrong, I'll own up to what I did and face the consequences. I'm the one they'll remember, since I doubt Tom will even recall you doing more than asking a few questions."

Keeping his eyes fixed upon Tom's still form, Baker sighed and nodded to himself. Every breath he took was coming to him easier than the one before it. "No. I did more than ask questions. I helped do this, so I'll own up to my part if that's what I have to do."

Clint walked up to him and placed a hand on Baker's shoulder. "Tom drew his gun on you and he meant to use it."

"I know he did."

"Besides, there is definitely something going on in Red Water. I can feel it in my bones and there's plenty of signs pointing to it. You must have seen a clue or two yourself, or you wouldn't have lent me a hand when I needed it."

"You're right," Baker said. "This didn't seem right from the moment I signed that damn book. I needed the money, though. Since none of the others saw fit to ask any questions, I guess I figured I'd just do my part and collect my pay. The marshal said it would only be for a few days, anyhow."

"Flynt knew how long you'd be gone?" Clint asked.

"Yeah." Baker squinted and added, "That does seem peculiar."

"Considering he didn't know where these outlaws were or when he would catch up to them, having any sort of schedule doesn't make any sense unless he wanted to get you men away from Red Water for that amount of time."

Clint looked down at Tom and studied him the way he might study a load of barrels that needed to be stacked onto an old wagon. "If you could just help me get him onto the back of my horse, I should be able to do the rest. No need for you to get in any deeper."

"What? You can't bring me in this far and just turn me loose now," Baker said.

"I shouldn't have brought you in at all. You're right. This could end up messy, but it could end up as nothing. Either way, you stand to lose more than me simply because you live around here and I can ride somewhere else when it's all said and done."

Baker walked around to Tom's feet and reached down for the bottom edge of the ropes that were wrapped around him. "Marshal Flynt's an asshole. His men are loudmouths that strut around like peacocks for no good reason. It won't be a surprise to anyone in Red Water to find out those men had their hands in some nasty business."

"You still have to live there. Ride away now and you can join up with the posse. Just do what you need to do, collect your fee, and—"

"Too late," Baker cut in. "I made up my mind. I was just a little shook up before but I'm better now."

"You are?" Clint asked.

"Yes."

Lifting Tom's upper half, Clint watched Baker closely. There was a difference in him now that he'd managed to wrap his head around what was going on. "So do you know a good spot we can leave Tom?"

"There's a field about a quarter mile outside of town. It's overrun with weeds and nobody's got any cause to go there. But if he gets loose, he'll be able to walk back into town before too long."

"That should be fine. Whatever is set to happen, my guess is that it'll start pretty soon."

"All right," Baker said. "Let's get moving."

TWENTY-EIGHT

Tom woke up somewhere along the way to the field outside of town. Since he was draped across Eclipse's rump, there wasn't much he could do other than squirm and thrash around like a grounded fish. The field was just as good as Baker had described, which meant it was actually fairly bad. By the looks of it, no one had raked or hoed that ground for years and the grass came up well past Clint's waist.

Baker and Clint hauled Tom to a spot in the middle of the field that was conveniently marked by a tattered old scarecrow. The post may have been weathered and covered with fungus, but it was still solid and had been sunk deeply into the ground. Clint anchored the deputy down well enough that the redhead couldn't find nearly enough leverage to get free anytime soon.

Stepping back, Clint was happy to see that the only visible sign of Tom's presence was a section of flattened grass at the base of the scarecrow. The weeds were thick and tall enough to cover the rest.

"Okay," Baker said. "I've dug myself in too far to crawl out now. What next?"

"There doesn't have to be anything next," Clint replied.

"Things are going to pan out pretty quickly or not at all. Either way, Flynt and his deputies will be exposed as incompetent liars if nothing else and you could get away with being my unwilling accomplice so far. Any further, and you're in for the whole stretch."

Baker nodded slowly and looked back to the part of the scarecrow that was sticking up above the weeds. Tom was obviously struggling, but the movement could easily be mistaken for the wind or some critters gnawing at the base of the post. Looking back at Clint, Baker asked, "You have a plan or are we just going to ride in more circles?"

"I've got a plan. In fact, I've already set a few lines in the water and there could be a nibble anytime."

"That's a hell of a lot more than Flynt offered. I'm in for the stretch."

Clint extended his hand. "I appreciate the help, Baker."

Before he shook the hand Clint was offering, Baker asked, "What exactly did you have in mind for me to do?"

"You remember the faces of those men from that wanted notice?"

"Yeah."

"Just keep looking for those faces as we go along," Clint said.

For a second, Baker seemed confused. He waited as if he were holding his breath in expectation of a gut punch. When the punch didn't come, he asked, "That's it?"

"There may be a bit more to it, but nothing more than what you'd expect when riding with a real posse."

Baker shrugged. "Fine, then. Let's go."

As they put the field behind them, Clint could hear the rustling of Tom's legs against the ground. To ears that didn't know any better, the sound could easily pass for an errant breeze.

TWENTY-NINE

Joan's Emporium was a quaint little place that could have passed for a shop selling any number of things. The sign didn't draw much attention to itself and the frilly curtains in the windows were always drawn. There was a neat row of flowers on either side of the walk leading up to the front door and the closest neighbor was twenty yards away. The Emporium was situated on the outskirts of a small town, so the owners were left alone to conduct their business as they saw fit.

They paid their taxes and they contributed to local functions. They took care of their own affairs and never asked for any extra attention from the law or anyone else. Anyone riding by might assume the place was anything from a dress shop to a fancy school. Stepping inside, a traveler would be greeted cordially and offered a refreshment. Unless the traveler was too rowdy or unsavory, they would enjoy another form of entertainment that was actually the specialty of the house.

The three men who walked into Joan's most recently were on the verge of being escorted to the door without getting the offer they'd been after. Fortunately, one of the men had a smooth enough manner to rectify the situation.

"Goodness, you ladies look lovely," Chris Jerrison said through a wide smile. His face was dirty and covered by thick, brushy stubble, but he carried himself as if he'd been scrubbed clean enough for Sunday mass.

Chris sat upon a padded sofa, while his two partners had picked out chairs in different spots around the sitting room. Also scattered throughout the room were women of various shapes and ages. All of them were dressed in formal attire, carefully eyeing the three men sipping the tea they'd been given.

The woman who'd provided the tea was older than the rest, but her long, silver hair flowed over her shoulders in a way that made her face seem regal. She nodded politely and said, "Thank you very much. You men look . . . well . . . I'm sure you're just fine under all that dust."

Grinning amiably, Chris shrugged. "It has been a long ride, to be certain."

Suddenly, the youngest of the three men set his teacup down and perched upon the edge of his rocking chair. "We didn't come here for tea and we didn't come to swap fancy talk. All we want is—"

"Excuse young Harvey," Chris interrupted. "We're all a bit frayed around the edges after our ride."

"I ain't frayed and don't call me Harvey!"

Samuel ground his teeth and Chris started to say something to counter what the younger man had blurted out, but was stopped short by one of the women who'd been standing on the edge of the room since the three men had arrived.

She was a tall blonde with a trim body that was wrapped in a cream-colored dress. High cheekbones, thin lips, and a pert little nose all came together to form a petite, friendly face. At the moment, her blue eyes were fixed directly upon the kid. "It's all right," she said as she reached down for his hand. "I can tell you're just a little wound up and I think I've got just the thing for it."

Caught in the middle of his fit, Harvey muttered, "You do?"

"Yes!" Chris said happily. "I believe all of us are wound up pretty tight."

After getting a subtle nod from the woman with the silver hair, two more ladies stepped forward from the group. One of them was a short woman in her twenties who looked as if she could be Spanish, Mexican, or even South American. Her exotic features and darker skin tone were warmly received by Chris when she stepped over to him and offered her hand. The woman who approached Samuel was the smallest of the bunch and had delicate, Chinese features that made her look like a doll. Samuel took her hand as gently as she'd offered it, which put a cute little smile upon her face.

"The ladies will discuss rates when you get to their rooms," the silver-haired woman explained. "You'll enjoy our baths, I'm sure. Lord knows you all need one."

Chris continued to talk to every woman in his sight and was practically dragged from the sitting room. Samuel spoke quietly to his escort. Harvey was nowhere to be found.

THIRTY

The blonde's room was one of the nicest the kid had ever seen. Every surface was covered with either pillows or lace and the air smelled like expensive perfume. As he'd been led there, he couldn't stop thinking about the softness of the arm wrapped around his or the silky touch of her hair when it brushed against his cheek. Now that they were alone, he practically swallowed his tongue. Fortunately, the blonde was more than ready to keep the silence from getting awkward.

"So," she said. "You don't like being called Harvey. What should I call you, then?"

"Folks call me Laramie," he said proudly.

She nodded as if she were genuinely impressed. "That sounds like a name you earned somehow."

The smirk on the kid's face widened, but he obviously held back from saying what first jumped to his mind. "I'm known for a few things," he told her. "And, yeah, I earned my name well enough."

"Well, I'm glad to meet you, Laramie. You can call me Pearl. It's not my real name either."

He nodded and shook her hand. "Pleased to meet ya."

Rather than let his hand go, she took it and placed it upon her hip. Even though her dress was modestly cut, it clung to her trim figure as though it had been drizzled onto her naked body. Moving his hand up and down along her side, she kept her eyes locked upon him and asked, "You like that, Laramie?"

"Y-yes, ma'am."

She grinned at the discomfort she was causing and then led him to the back of the room. A white bathtub sat in the corner, surrounded by small tables full of salts and powders. "How about I help you out of those clothes?" Not waiting for a response, she began to unbuckle and unbutton him until his clothes could be pulled off.

Laramie stood and nervously shifted on his feet. Although he was entranced by what Pearl was doing, he could only utter a few stuttering laughs and clipped words of encouragement.

Standing back and looking him up and down, she said, "Now pull those boots off and get in. I'll go fetch some hot water."

As soon as Pearl turned her back to him, Laramie hopped on one foot so he could pull the boot from the other. He nearly toppled sideways into the nearest table when he tried to switch feet, but managed to pull off the other boot without doing any damage to himself or the room.

The water in the tub was cool, but he got in anyway. Just as he was getting used to the chill, he saw Pearl walk back into the room carrying a bucket in each hand. She paused after shutting the door, set the buckets down, and then eased her dress off her shoulders. With a slow wriggle, she moved the dress all the way down to expose the gentle curve of her spine and the rounded lines of her tight, shapely buttocks. Her bare skin was every bit as smooth and pale as the name she'd chosen.

Pearl turned around and carried the buckets to the tub. She sat on the edge, dangling one leg into the water so Laramie could get a nice look at the golden tuft of hair between her thighs. Pouring the hot water into the tub, she said, "You like that. I can tell."

Laramie self-consciously leaned forward to cover up his growing erection. He was even too flustered to object when Pearl emptied a portion of scented salts into the water before adding the second bucket.

"Scrub up now," she purred. "I'll wait for you over here." With that, Pearl walked slowly over to the bed, twitching her hips every step of the way. When she got there, she turned and lowered herself so she was sitting on the edge of the mattress. Pearl closed her eyes and let out a soft moan as she slipped her hand between her legs and started rubbing.

Laramie watched her for a few seconds but once she started tracing quick circles over her clitoris, he couldn't start scrubbing fast enough. After a quick, thorough bath, he practically jumped out of the tub and rushed over to the bed.

Slowly opening her eyes, Pearl smiled and stood up to greet him. "That's better," she said as she took in the sight of his dripping body. Picking up a towel, she started at his chest and then dried him off all the way down to his feet.

Pearl remained on her knees and looked up at him. "Now that you're all clean . . ." she whispered. Rather than finish what she was saying, she let her actions speak for herself. Pearl's thin lips parted and she placed them gently around his stiff penis. Resting her hands upon his legs, she slowly licked him and moaned softly from the back of her throat so he could feel it all the way down to his toes.

Before long, Laramie couldn't help but breathe quicker and grunt louder. His muscles tensed and he reached down to grab hold of Pearl's head. She read him like a book and calmly pulled away from him while getting to her feet. Ig-

noring the intensity in his eyes, she moved him to the bed
and told him, "Lay back."

Laramie did as he was told. Every fiber in his body
wanted to finish what she'd started, but he wasn't disappointed by the way she'd shifted gears. As soon as he'd
scooted up onto the bed and stretched out, Pearl was climbing on top of him. She crawled like a cat, allowing her long
hair to fall forward and brush against his stomach and chest
as she straddled his hips.

"Are you ready for me?" she asked as she rubbed her
pussy up and down against his cock.

"Hell, yes, I am."

She smiled, closed her eyes, and sat upright with her
palms flat against his stomach. Pearl continued to slide
against him until the lips between her legs became wet and
all she needed to do was shift her hips to fit him between
them. When she lowered herself on him, they both let out
grateful sighs.

Laramie's eyes were wide as saucers and he lay perfectly still while Pearl started to rock slowly back and forth
on top of him.

"You like that?" she asked.

Since he couldn't quite speak, Laramie nodded.

She kept her eyes closed and arched her back as she
picked up her pace. Pearl's upper body swayed just enough
to get her pert breasts moving. Small, pink nipples became
erect as she started grinding her hips back and forth.

Her rhythm was slow and easy, causing her lower body
to pump with an almost hypnotic motion while her upper
body remained quite still. Laramie watched her for a while
before he finally reached up to put his hands on her hips.
She responded to him immediately by letting out a moan
and throwing her hair over her shoulders. Emboldened by
that, Laramie thrust up into her.

Pearl let out a groan that filled the room and ran her hands over his chest. Clenching her eyes shut even tighter, she stopped rocking on him and started to bounce. She moved faster and faster, dropping down harder each time. Her breasts shook enticingly as her nipples became fully erect.

As much as Laramie wanted to grab hold of her and feel every last part of her body, it was all he could do just to keep from exploding. He couldn't slow his breathing down or think about anything else other than how tight and wet Pearl felt as she gripped his cock and rode it all the way up and all the way back down again.

"That's it," she moaned softly. "Just like that."

And, just like that, Laramie was past the point of no return.

Despite the fact that he was the one lying on his back, he felt as if he'd ridden for a few miles on the back of a bucking bronco. He emptied himself inside her and could hardly breathe for a full minute afterward. In that time, Pearl had opened her eyes and climbed off him.

"That was nice," she said as she walked over to the wall next to the bed and grabbed a robe hanging from a hook there. She pulled the robe on, but didn't bother tying it shut. That way, her pert breasts were covered, but the wet thatch of blond hair between her legs could still be seen.

Laramie thought of plenty he could say, but didn't have the breath for it. Instead, he rubbed his eyes and shifted on the soft blanket.

Someone knocked on the door, so Pearl strode over to answer it. "That might be Gertrude," she said as she casually closed her robe. "She'll want to collect your money."

Laramie didn't bother opening his eyes. He just listened to the squeak of the door's hinges, followed by a voice that was much too rough to have come from the woman with the silver hair in the sitting room.

"If you two are finished, I'd like to have a word with that fella."

Laramie's eyes snapped open. He saw the smooth lines of Pearl's back before she stepped aside to reveal Clint standing in the doorway.

"Throw some clothes on, kid," Clint said. "And leave the gun on the floor."

THIRTY-ONE

Clint stepped into the room and looked around. "Someone told me this was the nicest cathouse in the county. Looks to me like they were right."

"This isn't a cathouse," Pearl stated. "We entertain our gentlemen as we see fit."

"Pardon me," Clint said as he allowed himself to admire Pearl's trim body. "Someone from Tanner Hall steered me here and they lumped this place in with the other cat—emporiums in the area." Shifting his eyes to Laramie, he added, "But nobody needed to tell me that a young buck like you wouldn't wait long before calling on a place like this."

Laramie squirmed on the bed. He'd pulled a blanket around to cover himself, but he didn't have it in him to stand up and expose himself further to an armed man. Trying his best to keep his voice from wavering, he asked, "How'd you know I'd be here?"

"I didn't. I just had a hunch and put the word out to a few folks to keep their eyes open for someone like you and your partners to pay them a visit."

"That damn old bitch," Laramie snarled through gritted teeth.

Clint lunged forward to grab the kid by the chin. "Keep your tough talk to yourself. I want to know what you're doing here."

"What the hell do you think I'm doing?"

Nodding slowly as he backed up a step, Clint glanced at Pearl and asked, "You mind giving me and the kid the room for a few minutes? I need to have a word with him and it may not be suitable for the ears of a lady."

Still appalled at the way Laramie had spoken about the silver-haired madam of the house, Pearl wrapped her robe around herself even tighter and replied, "Just don't leave a mess. From my experience, though, you won't need much time before he's all done anyway."

Laramie shook his head and started to mutter something to Pearl's back, but stopped short when he saw the warning glare from Clint.

"Don't get too worked up, kid," Clint said. "You play your cards right and you may just live long enough to get some more practice where women are concerned."

"Can I get dressed, or are you admiring the view?"

"I told you to put some clothes on before, but you were too scared to move." Sliding his boot beneath a rumpled pair of jeans, Clint kicked them to Laramie. "Here you go."

As he shoved his legs into his jeans, Laramie kept a scowl on his face and glared at Clint. Even though Clint wasn't shaking under the petulant stare, Laramie kept it going anyhow.

"So you're Laramie, huh? I heard that other one call you Harvey."

"Everyone calls me Laramie," he spat.

"Why's that?" Clint asked.

"On account of all the trains I robbed that were going through Wyoming."

"Oh, so you're a robber. What are you planning to rob here in Red Water?"

Widening his smirk a bit more, the kid grunted, "Wouldn't you like to know?"

"Yeah," Clint replied as he reached down to pick up the kid's weathered Cavalry model six-shooter. "I would. And you're going to tell me before I lose my patience."

"If you were the law, you would'a shown yer badge by now. If you were a bounty hunter, you wouldn't give a rat's ass what I was doing or why I was here." With every point he made, Laramie edged closer to the side of the bed. By the time he settled his feet on the floor, he seemed to have regained most of his confidence. "And if you meant to use that gun of yours, you would'a skinned it already."

With that, Laramie launched off the bed and flew at Clint. His arms were outstretched and his lips were parted in a vicious snarl.

Clint stood his ground just long enough for Laramie to commit himself, then stepped aside at the last second. When Laramie got within arm's reach, Clint dropped one fist down on the younger man's back like he was pounding a railroad spike into the ground.

Laramie let out a grunt and landed on his belly. Before he even realized he was on Clint's boot, he felt the boot come straight up to flop him onto his back. Clint looked down at him and shook his head.

Sitting up, Laramie reached for the pistol in Clint's hand. He wasn't fast enough to get ahold of the weapon before it was pulled away. He scrambled to his feet, looked up, but couldn't find Clint. Suddenly, he felt a hand drop onto his shoulder and turn him around. Clint's fist slammed into Laramie's mouth, knocking his head back and sending him staggering toward the bed.

"That," Clint told him, "was for trying to steal my horse.

Now you'll either tell me what you're doing here in Red Water or things are bound to get a lot worse."

"Go to hell." Laramie grunted.

Clint rushed forward and shoved Laramie with enough force to send him toppling off the opposite side of the bed. As the kid tried to get his feet beneath him again, Clint walked around the bed and said, "Horse thieves are hanged just about anywhere. While I doubt you're some known man or a train robber, I know you're a horse thief. I'll bet there are plenty of folks around here who would love to stretch that neck of yours."

Laramie crouched on the floor with his back against the wall. As soon as he saw Clint again, he growled, "Ain't nobody's been able to catch me!"

Clint was prepared for the kid to take another run at him, so he'd tensed his stomach and planted his feet to prepare for the impact. Laramie's shoulder slammed against him and the kid's bare feet continued to scrape against the floor. Even though Clint maintained the upper hand so far, he was losing his grip on Laramie's gun.

When he saw Laramie trying to grab the modified Colt from him, Clint looped one arm down and across the kid's chest so he could lift him up. Just to be safe, Clint swept one leg straight back to send the Cavalry model gun skidding toward the door.

It was an awkward struggle, but Clint was strong enough to get the job done. The fact that Laramie's legs cracked against the wall and bed frame also served to slow him down a bit as the bruises kept piling on top of each other.

"You . . . might as well come clean, kid," Clint said as he continued to wrestle with Laramie. "Tell me what I want to know and I might just . . ."

Sneaking in a punch that Clint hadn't braced for, Laramie was able to wriggle free and stagger away. He spotted his gun lying on the floor and dove for it. This time, he'd been fast enough to make his move before Clint could stop him. Unfortunately, his own momentum sent him reeling across the room until he knocked against a wall.

Before Laramie could take aim, Clint drew his Colt and thumbed back the hammer. The motion wasn't necessary to fire the weapon, but the metallic click of the mechanism was more than enough to freeze the kid in his tracks.

"You're right about one thing," Clint said. "I could have killed you already if that was my intention, but I can still do it the moment you become more trouble than you're worth."

Swearing under his breath, Laramie opened his hand and allowed his gun to hit the floor.

"I already heard plenty from Marshal Flynt," Clint said. "Perhaps you can tell me enough to warrant putting him away instead of you."

"The only one going away will be you. Chris and Samuel will gun you down as soon as you step foot outside this door."

"Really? So they just let you get knocked around for a laugh? Or maybe they didn't hear any commotion? I'm sure they stuck around to make certain you weren't in any trouble, even if it meant they'd get themselves caught along the way."

Judging by the darkening expression on Laramie's face, he wasn't having any trouble whatsoever picking up on the point Clint was making. As more seconds ticked by without any trace of help arriving, the kid's face only grew darker.

THIRTY-TWO

Clint could hear footsteps racing down the hall the instant he kicked open the door. Keeping one hand locked around the back of Laramie's neck, with his other hand he jammed the barrel of his Colt into the horse thief's back and leaned forward to take a peek into the hall. When he saw who was racing to the room, he shoved the kid out in front of him and then stepped outside himself.

"What is the meaning of all this commotion?" the silver-haired woman asked. "I demand to know or I'll put all of you men out on your ears!"

Pearl emerged from one of the other rooms and hurried to intercept the older woman before she got to Clint. "It's all right, Gertrude."

The silver-haired madam turned her eyes toward the blonde, but it didn't do much to lessen the anger written all over her face. "It's a long cry from all right! It sounded like those two tore the room down!"

"Don't you remember Clint?" Pearl asked. "He came by this morning to let us know that those horse thieves might be coming by."

Swatting at the blonde as if she were swatting a fly, Gertrude replied, "Of course I remember! That's why I allowed those filthy men into my house. But I didn't agree to let him destroy my rooms and I sure didn't agree to let those animals break my windows!"

"What windows?" Clint asked.

"The windows in the two rooms where those other two were being entertained," the old woman shot back. "First I heard you two tussling in there and then I heard glass shattering! I couldn't catch those two before they lit out of here, but I sure as hell can catch you!"

Clint looked at the kid in his custody and was surprised he didn't see steam shooting from his ears. Laramie's face was red and his teeth were clamped tight enough to crack every last one of them.

"And," Gertrude continued, "they took off without paying me a dime!"

By now, the hall was filled with women. Clint didn't think any of them would make any wrong moves, but he was getting awfully distracted by all the pretty faces and ample curves on display. Before his mind was diverted too much further, he focused on Gertrude and said, "I intend on paying for all the damages."

"You're damn right you are!"

"And there's a bonus in it for you if I could ask one more favor."

The silver-haired woman gnawed on the inside of her cheek, crossed her arms sternly, and asked, "How much of a bonus and what kind of favor?"

"Do you have a cellar?"

"Just a small one where we keep food and some old furniture."

"If I could impose on you to use your cellar to keep this young man here from getting away or being discovered by his partners, I'd make sure you get paid an additional hundred dollars for your trouble."

For the first time since she'd stormed down the hall, Gertrude looked as if she wasn't going to wring someone's neck. Even though her temper had eased up a bit, there was still a sharp edge to her voice when she asked, "Is that on top of what my girls earned?"

"And the damages, yes, ma'am."

Now Gertrude actually smiled. "I can keep quiet about this, but my girls aren't armed guards."

"I brought along a friend to watch over him."

Pearl nodded. "Baker's waiting outside."

"So you men really are part of the marshal's posse?" Gertrude asked.

Clint nodded. "That's right. Even so, I'd be obliged if nobody let anyone know about our arrangement, and that includes the marshal or his deputies."

"No skin off my nose," the older woman replied with another wave of her hand. "The only thing those lawmen are good for is sniffing around here for a free roll in one of my girls' beds every couple of weeks. They're the reason I had to set up just outside of Red Water instead of the prime spot I had on Sales Street. But you should know one thing, Clint. I may be old, but I can still beat the tar out of someone who tries to cheat me out of my money."

"I don't doubt that, ma'am."

"Good," she said as she slipped back into the cordial tone that Laramie recognized when she'd served him and the others tea in the sitting room. "Pearl will show you to the cellar. You need anything else, just let me know."

During the whole conversation, Clint had been expecting Laramie to kick, holler, try to throw a punch, or do anything to get away from him. As more women had gathered in the hall to see what was going on, Clint had been afraid the horse thief might try to grab one of them as a bargaining chip to get out of the house.

But Laramie hadn't done any of those things. In fact, all he did while being led through the house was hang from the end of Clint's hand like a dead carp dangling from the end of a fishing line. All Clint had to do to keep the kid moving was nudge him in the back with the barrel of his Colt.

"Well, now," Clint said as a way to point out what Laramie already knew, "looks like your partners aren't coming for you after all."

Pearl shot a quick look over her shoulder and then turned to lead them through a well-stocked kitchen. The little bit of pity in her eyes was enough to make Laramie's head hang low.

"They're after the safes." Laramie grunted.

Clint chuckled and steered the kid toward the back door. "Sure. I do recall seeing a lot of big banks around here. You'll have to do better than that."

"They're not in any damn banks. They're being made by some old man who works around here."

"Oh," Clint replied as the picture came into focus. "Those safes."

THIRTY-THREE

Watching Clint tie Laramie to a solid oak chair, Baker seemed ready to squirm out of his skin. It only made him more nervous to be crouched down in a root cellar that was roughly triple the size of a grave. The walls were lined with shelves, and various chairs and tables were stacked all the way up to the six-foot-high ceiling.

"Were them others in there?" Baker asked.

"They were, but they're gone now," Clint replied.

"Are you sure about that?"

"I'm sure."

Laramie sagged against the ropes holding him to the back of the chair and grumbled another string of obscenities.

Once the knots were tightened and a rag was stuffed into Laramie's mouth, Clint turned his back on the kid and left him in the squared hole in the ground. Then Clint pushed Baker out of the cellar, followed him out, and shut the door. They stood just a few paces away from the back porch of Joan's Emporium. It was a good-sized, well-maintained house just outside of the Red Water limits and far enough away for Clint to get a good look at most of the town. The cellar entrance looked like a squat outhouse set on the upper slope of a little hill not far from the real outhouse.

Dropping his voice to a whisper, Clint said, "I'm not sure if those men are gone or not."

"But you just said—"

Baker was cut short when Clint pushed him even farther away from the cellar entrance. "That was for the kid's benefit," Clint explained. "Now that he thinks he's been left by his friends, he'll be more likely to throw some grief their way. That's where I come in."

"You mean we?"

"No. All you need to do is stay here and make sure the kid doesn't get away. Just look in on him every now and then, but don't get too close. He may still have a wild hair or two."

Nodding, Baker couldn't stop looking back and forth between the main house and the little shack built over the narrow steps that led into the root cellar. "So you really knew those men would come here?"

Clint smirked and said, "It was a hunch. Remember those lines I told you I cast?"

"Yeah."

"I cast them right before riding out of town. I had a hunch those horse thieves were close and guessed they might stop in for some companionship while waiting for whatever it was Flynt had in mind. I rode to the cathouses here in town and spread the word that I would pay for information regarding the men if they stopped by. It cost me a few dollars at every place I went to, but it was worth it."

"That's where you went to when you left the posse for a little bit this morning?"

Clint nodded. "I started at Tanner Hall, just because that seemed to be Flynt's second home. Someone there told me about the other cathouses in Red Water and it wasn't long before I was steered to this place."

"So you knew they would be coming back to town even before Tom confirmed it."

"I was going to do the same thing at any other nearby towns, but I got lucky with this one. I may have seen those men only for a short while the first time, but that kid looked like the sort that would hightail it to a cathouse before going to a saloon. Besides, cathouses are easier to hide in. Like I said, it was a hunch. Fortunately, we don't need to take another gamble to figure out what that kid's two friends have in mind."

"Yeah? So where are we going next?"

Clint placed his hand on Baker's shoulder and told him, "Just me, Baker."

But Baker was already shaking his head. "I'm a member of this posse just like you are. Just because the marshal and his deputies aren't here . . . that means you need my help more than anything."

"That's right and you'll be a big help by keeping an eye on the kid in there. Make sure he doesn't budge from the cellar and that nobody finds out he's here."

"And . . . what about the marshal?" Baker asked. "He's bound to come back sooner or later. What do I tell him?"

"I'm not sure just yet, but I think that will sort itself out when everything else gets dragged into the open."

THIRTY-FOUR

Clint was counting on the fact that Marshal Flynt could at least get a few things right. For one, clearing the town of anyone who might take a stand against anyone like Laramie or his partners was supposedly the lawman's top priority. Therefore, Clint hoped he could ride down the streets of Red Water without anyone of note taking an interest in him.

Second, Clint had to assume the lawmen might post a few eyes here and there, so he couldn't take the chance of riding directly to the front door of Franklin Fixtures. He climbed down from his saddle a few avenues away from the one he was after and then led Eclipse a bit farther down Sales Street. Once he got close enough, Clint tied Eclipse to a hitching post and kept his head angled so the brim of his hat covered a good portion of his face.

While Flynt's sense of organizing a posse seemed lackluster at best, the marshal seemed to have a time line for following through with his real plan. Unfortunately for the lawman, Clint's arrival and scuffle at Joan's Emporium had very likely bumped Flynt's schedule up a bit. These things and several others tore through Clint's mind in the same way statistics came and went during a poker game. Certain things factored into a win, others pointed toward a loss.

For the moment, at least, Clint liked his chances.

He hurried down Franklin Avenue as quickly as he could without drawing attention to himself. It was a busy time of the afternoon and there were plenty of shops in the area, so Clint had more than enough of a crowd to use as cover. But there could just as easily be men hiding in the crowd to look for someone like him.

By the time he got to Franklin Fixtures, Clint had yet to spot anyone who seemed too suspicious. Even so, he kept his hand near his Colt as he stepped into the shop.

"Clint? Is that you?"

Wincing at just how quickly he'd been spotted, Clint shut the door and walked over to the counter. Of course, he couldn't be too surprised that Allie had picked him out right away. She had seen an awful lot of him since he'd been in Red Water.

"Yeah," he told her, "it's me."

She rushed around the counter and gave him a quick kiss on the cheek. "That's going to have to do for now," she whispered. "I can't exactly close up and give you the same service you had last time."

"It's all right. I'm here on business." He placed a hand at the small of her back and guided her away from the front door. Although Allie squirmed a bit, she went along with him.

"Hold on a moment. Is the posse back already?"

"Not just yet. Are there any customers in here?"

"Not right now." Allie planted her feet halfway down the aisle that led to the back of the shop and refused to budge. "What's going on, Clint? Don't tell me it's nothing, because I already know better than that. You're acting strange."

"Has anyone been in this shop today?" he asked.

"I won't say another word until you tell me what's wrong."

The shop was small enough that Clint could see the entire section where any customers might be. The front was taken up mostly by the sales counter and cash register, while the rest had various samples scattered about on the walls or on small tables. There were a few cases along one wall and the back was the open area that he, Allie, and Gwen had gotten to know not too long ago.

"It's about those men we were after," he explained. "They might be in town."

"Well, I haven't left the store since opening."

"That's the thing," Clint continued. "I think they might intend on coming here if they haven't been here already."

Just as Clint had feared, Allie didn't take that news too well. Her face paled and she reached up to place her hand flat over her heart. "Oh, Lord." She sighed.

"I already got one of them," he told her as a way to calm her down a bit. "But the other two are still about. One is a black fellow that's a little bigger than me. The other is around my size with a narrower face. Both of them are in their early thirties or so. Have you seen anyone like that?"

"A man like the first one you described came by to check on a few prices, but that was over a week ago."

"What did he look like?"

Allie closed her eyes and clenched her lips shut as if she were trying to dig up the memory from a dusty corner of her mind. She shook her head and said, "I just remember he was black. He might have been bigger than you, but that's it. Oh, and I think he was wearing a dress coat."

"A dress coat?"

"That's right," she said definitely. "I remember it because it was a formal coat and he wore buckskins under it. That was peculiar."

Clint smiled as if he'd been dealt the missing card to fill an inside straight. "Perfect. Do you recall what he wanted?"

"He asked about building a safe. I gave him some prices, but he didn't seem to know exactly what he wanted. I passed him along to Sven."

The smile on Clint's face dimmed when he heard that. "And that was a week ago?"

"Maybe a little more."

"And," Clint asked reluctantly, "have you heard from Sven since then?"

Allie started nodding right away. "Oh, yes. I don't even think he spoke to that man for more than a few minutes, but it went off without a hitch."

"What's Sven working on now?"

"I know he's working on a few orders, but he may be doing that in his own workshop because I haven't seen him all day."

"Is that unusual?"

"Not really," she told him. "I don't even see him unless there's his sort of work to be done. Hold on a second, though." Allie walked back to the front of the store before Clint could make a move. He followed along behind her and kept walking to the front window when she stopped at the front counter.

Clint stood so he was able to look out the front window while being mostly veiled by the simple brown curtain that covered it. Pushing the curtain aside a bit with his finger, Clint peeked out onto Franklin Avenue to find nothing more than a steady flow of people wandering up and down the narrow road.

"That's odd," Allie said.

Looking at her, Clint saw Allie peering into an open ledger and tracing something with the tip of her finger. "What's odd?" he asked.

"Sven was supposed to be in the shop today. He was working on a commission and he needed to use the equipment here."

"What equipment?"

Allie was already walking around the counter again and striding toward the back of the shop. Motioning for him to follow, she said, "It's all back here. He's probably just busy and forgot to say hello."

Clint was quick to catch up to her and even got in front of Allie before she reached the back door. He reached ahead of her and said, "Allow me."

She stepped back and let him open the door. Outside, there was a small shed, which was kept shut by a large metal lock. The shed was too small for anyone to work inside with the door closed unless that person was a little child hoping to win a game of hide-and-seek.

"That's odd," Allie said again.

"Lock up the store," Clint told her. "Then take me to Sven's house."

THIRTY-FIVE

Sven lived at the other end of Sales Street off Homestead Avenue. It was easy enough to see where the road had gotten its name since the only buildings on both sides of the narrow path were houses with enough stable space to accommodate the horses of the folks who lived in them. Apart from a few larger places at the far end of the street where the town thinned out, the homes were short and narrow. Some structures were two floors high, connected by rickety stairs that seemed ready to fall off the sides of the homes to which they were nailed.

"There," Allie said as she pointed to the second floor atop one of the rickety sets of stairs. "That's where Sven lives."

Clint surveyed the road and didn't like what he saw. There were so many houses stacked on both sides that any number of people could be watching from any vantage point. There were rooftops riflemen could use to pick someone off from a distance. There were doorways bushwhackers could lurk waiting for the right moment to strike. The more Clint looked around, the more he wanted to forget about climbing those shaky stairs. Unfortunately, Allie wasn't quite so reluctant.

"Come on," she said as she walked toward the bottom of the stairs and waved for him to follow. "I'll show you to his room."

Clint walked behind her, but wanted to get in front in case someone was waiting at the top of the stairs for them. Before he could get around her, he reconsidered, thinking he should stay behind in case someone tried to rush up after them. Since he could see the street, but not the room at the top of the stairs, he went with his first instinct.

"Allow me," he said as he reached past her to grab the door handle.

Allie smiled and bowed her head to allow him to walk past her and into the room.

The door came open easily, and indeed seemed about ready to fall off its hinges. Clint stepped inside and took in his surroundings as quickly as his darting eyes would allow. There wasn't much to see, so he was able to size it up in a matter of seconds.

The front door opened to a small room that had a little table and a pair of chairs. There was a single cabinet, a crate of utensils, and a broom propped in the corner. A narrow door opened to another room, which probably was a bedroom. Clint couldn't see much through that door because of the spindly man walking through it.

Hunching down to fit through the door, the man reminded Clint of the scarecrow that he'd left to guard Tom. Matted bunches of dark blond hair sprouted at odd angles from his scalp to partially cover a shriveled face. Clint would have guessed the man's age at anywhere from thirty to fifty.

"What is this?" the man rasped in a thick Swedish accent. "Who you are?"

Clint felt Allie behind him, so he stepped aside to let her in. When he saw the man reach for a gun he'd kept inside the bedroom, Clint extended his arm to keep Allie from getting in the way. Before he could draw his Colt, he felt Allie press against his arm.

"Sven, it's me!" she said.

Lifting his chin and squinting, the blond man seemed to be gazing through a thick fog. "Allison? Who this man is?"

Allie impatiently pushed Clint's arm up enough for her to duck under it. "This is Clint," she replied. "He's a friend of mine."

"Your friend doesn't know how to knock."

"No," Allie said as she shot an accusing glare at Clint. "He sure doesn't. Sorry about that."

Clint took a look outside and didn't see anyone in the immediate area who hadn't been there before. Of course, that wasn't accounting for all the hiding spaces that he couldn't make out no matter how hard he tried. "There are some suspicious men about," Clint said. "Did anyone pay you a visit recently?"

Sven scowled at Clint and then looked at Allie.

"You know what I mean by suspicious?" Clint asked.

Scowling even harder at Clint, Sven replied, "Yes, I know what this means. I have been in this country for little while."

"You recall that man who came by a week or so ago to ask about building those safes?" Allie asked.

Sven nodded right away. "Yes. The fellow with the dark skin. He did not want any safes built. I know this because he did not even know what to ask when I gave him my valuable time."

"What do you mean by that?" Clint asked.

Slowing his speech down as if he were talking to a weak-minded child, Sven replied, "I ask him about tumblers, multiple backings, and how many bolts he wants to hold the door closed. You know what I mean by these things?"

"Sort of," Clint admitted.

Despite the vagueness in Clint's voice, Sven grinned and opened his arms as if he'd been shown an epiphany. "Yes! Just like this. When I talk to this dark man from before, he look at me just like this. He was more interested in what I do before and what I am going to deliver yesterday."

Clint shook his head as if something had suddenly come loose between his ears. Although English words were coming out of Sven's mouth, they were just disconnected enough to make Clint work extra hard to put them together. Suddenly, a few tumblers fell into place within Clint's head. "Oh, you mean that safe that was picked up from your shop yesterday?"

"Ah, maybe perhaps you are not so slow as I thought," Sven replied.

"What did he want to know about that?"

"Yeah," Allie said. "What did he want to know about our deliveries?"

"Just who else was buying and what they wanted and things like this and such."

Allie shook her head. "I wish you would have said that before, Sven. That's important."

"I know this is important. He wants to know what work I do and if I can be trusted for more work somewhere else."

"Please tell me you didn't talk about the other bank orders," Allie begged.

Sven tapped his temple and gave her a quick wink. "I know better than this. I tell him other banks, so he doesn't know which I have the work for."

Clint rolled his eyes and let out an exasperated breath. He may not understand everything the other man was saying, but he'd heard more than enough. "That's what they're after, all right. If any bank robber worth his salt got ahold of the plans for those safes or the man who put them together, it'd make getting into them a whole lot easier, wouldn't it?"

"Sure," Sven replied. "But I keep my plans hidden well. They would need to shoot me dead to get a look at . . ." His voice tapered off when he saw Clint's raised eyebrow and slow nod. "Oh. I see what you are saying."

"And after they turned this place upside down to get those plans," Clint explained, "all they'd need to do is wait to see who picks up the safes and follow them to wherever they're bound."

"Then they'd wait for them to fill up with money and steal them back again." Allie sighed.

Launching into a burst of nervous motion, Sven moved to the nearby cupboards and pulled out pots, pans, and whatever else was in there. "We should call sheriff or marshal or federals or . . ."

"There's nobody here," Clint said. "That's the point."

"Then we need to leave! I have gun, but—"

Allie stopped him with a gentle hand on his shoulder. "That's why we're here, Sven. Forget the pans and just collect a few things you'll need for a few days."

"And the plans for those safes," Clint added.

Sven tapped his forehead again, but aimed his wink at Clint. "I already think of this. My things are kept in here beneath the oatmeal." Grabbing a dented canister, he held it out for the other two to see and then promptly tossed it away. "Oatmeal. Here are the plans," Sven announced as he picked up a stack of papers that was wide enough after being folded in half to cover the entire shelf like a liner.

"Is that all?" Clint asked.

"Yes, but the safes are in my workshop."

"You think they'll try to steal those?" Allie asked.

Clint shrugged. "I wouldn't think that would do them

any good, but they might be desperate enough to try hitting the shop to see what else they can find."

"If no law in town and posse is off somewhere," Sven pointed out, "why would they try to rob fixture shop?"

Clint froze as a cold feeling ripped through him. "Aww, hell." He snarled.

THIRTY-SIX

Clint led the way down the rickety stairs, but didn't expect to see either of the two outlaws out there waiting to strike. While there was still the possibility of running into them, there were just too many other possibilities in Red Water. The town was open. The longer Clint thought about what he would do in the boots of the two outlaws, the more he scolded himself for not thinking about such things before.

But there was still a plan at work and Clint reminded himself that the outlaws in question weren't the sharpest knives in the drawer. For that reason alone, he went back to Franklin Fixtures before going anywhere else. Once Franklin Avenue was in sight, Clint stopped and looked at the two people following him.

"Is there anywhere you can go that's safe?" Clint asked Allie. "Somewhere that others might not know about?"

"I can go to Gwen's," she replied.

"What about someplace that might not drag anyone else into this mess?"

"Gwen's not going to be there for a while," Allie explained. "She headed out to Dodge City this morning. That's why she was so . . ." Glancing quickly over to Sven, Allie blushed and said, "That's why she wanted to pack in so much celebrating over Founder's Day."

"All right," Clint said hastily. Shifting his eyes to Sven, he asked, "You brought those guns of yours, right?"

"Oh, yes."

"Then you take Allie to Gwen's, lock the door, and wait for me to come get you. First, hand over those plans."

Sven's eyes narrowed and he reflexively pressed a hand against the outside of the coat pocket where the folded papers were being kept.

"It's best if I keep them, so there's no reason for them to come looking for you," Clint explained. It wasn't the most convincing thing he could come up with, but the blond man nodded and handed them over.

"Because you are a friend of Allison and you are a duly appointed—"

"Great," Clint said as he took the plans Sven offered and stuffed them into his own pocket. "We don't have a lot of time, so make yourselves scarce and don't show your faces until it's safe. Now where's Gwen's place?"

"Right down the street," Allie said.

Clint was hoping for as much, since Sales Street led to nearly every other spot in Red Water. "Go on now. I'll keep an eye on you."

Allie nodded and practically shoved Sven along in front of her as she crossed the street and picked up speed. Sven stumbled awkwardly without looking where he was going and almost broke his neck a few times, since he seemed more concerned with patting down his pockets than putting one foot in front of the other.

Keeping his head down and his hands stuffed in his pockets, Clint watched the duo weave through the folks walking down Sales Street. If there were more than two outlaws on the loose, he wouldn't have been so quick to let

Allie and Sven go. But not only were the outlaws working with low numbers, they were also probably getting desperate and sloppy.

Before Clint could try to make a guess as to how sloppy the outlaws might be, he saw one of them make the very move he'd been hoping for.

Chris Jerrison kept his head down as he stepped out from behind a group of men gathered in front of a saloon. Fortunately, he'd been in a bit too much of a hurry to catch up to Allie, and by racing in a straight line for her and Sven, he made picking him out of the crowd that much easier.

Clint, on the other hand, wasn't worried about blending into the crowd. Now that Chris had tipped his hand, Clint was perfectly content to announce himself if it meant giving Allie and Sven a running head start. He just prayed that those two would take advantage of it.

"Hey!" Clint shouted when he realized he still hadn't caught Chris's eye.

Not only did his shout catch Jerrison's eye, but it also drew some gunfire. From where Clint was standing, he couldn't see the gun in Chris's hand. But he sure as hell saw it when the outlaw brought the weapon up and fired a few quick shots.

Clint dove toward the other side of the street and reached for his modified Colt. Now that the shooting had started, he knew he was the only one in town who could put a stop to it.

THIRTY-SEVEN

Hot lead blazed through the air, causing folks on the street to scream and scatter in all directions. A few of the locals dropped and covered their heads with their hands, but Clint had already circled around them to get a better angle on his target.

He cleared leather and pulled his trigger in a single, fluid motion. The Colt bucked against Clint's palm and sent a round toward Jerrison. But Chris wasn't about to stand still to catch the bullet. Instead, he ducked down low and made a mad dash back toward Franklin Avenue. Since that was on the opposite side of Sales Street from where Allie and Sven were headed, Clint was more than willing to let Chris go.

Once he had a clear line of sight, Clint fired a few more rounds to keep Chris moving in the proper direction. Sure enough, the outlaw ducked down Franklin Avenue and fired wildly to cover his retreat. With Chris in front of him and Allie at his back, Clint replaced the spent rounds in his pistol with ones from his gun belt and ran into the fray.

More screams came from Franklin Avenue, but the bullets were still aimed at Clint. He could tell as much by the occasional sound of lead whipping through the air or the sight of splinters shot off a wall at the mouth of the avenue. Clint arrived at the corner and pressed his back against one of the buildings. He then chanced a look down Franklin Avenue by leaning quickly for a peek.

With folks scattering or diving for cover, it was fairly easy to pick out Jerrison. The outlaw kept his back to another wall and unleashed a fiery hailstorm the moment he caught sight of Clint.

"That you, Adams?" Chris called out. "You just don't know when to quit, do ya?"

Clint smirked and replied, "You're about to be surrounded, so why not just give it up?"

"Give it up?" Jerrison replied. "Surrounded? You sure about that? Do you think I'm stupid enough to—"

"Nope," Clint muttered to himself as he bolted for the door of the building he was up against that was facing Sales Street. "But I sure hope you keep talking for a while."

Clint wasn't able to make out what Jerrison was saying, but he could hear the outlaw shouting from Franklin Avenue. Every so often, another few shots were fired.

Rather than stand aside and try to guess where every bullet was going, Clint raced through what appeared to be a clothing shop. After entering through the Sales Street door, he ran straight down the aisle that led all the way to the rear of the place. When he got to the back of the shop, Clint found himself surrounded by men's suits on racks and a very confused tailor.

Clint pointed to a stout wooden door and asked, "Does that door open onto Franklin Avenue?"

The tailor shook his head. "That just leads to the lot out back. You can see Franklin from there and you could—"

"Thanks," Clint said hastily as he opened the door and ran outside.

Sure enough, there was a small lot piled high with empty

crates next to a two-seater outhouse. Clint got his bearings and looked to his right. The lot was surrounded by a waist-high fence and beyond that was another road. Since the sound of a gunshot came from that road, Clint guessed it was Franklin Avenue.

"Where you hidin', Adams?" Jerrison shouted from somewhere a bit farther down Franklin. "I know all about you and you didn't strike me as the sort to take off like a scalded dog."

Clint ran as fast as he could while also trying to keep his steps from making too much noise. He needed to sacrifice a bit of speed, but Clint was able to hop a fence and circle around another building to work his way a little farther down Franklin. When he looked around that other building, Clint could see the edge of Franklin Fixtures and could hear Chris's voice a little more clearly, as if nearer.

He could even catch a few words that Jerrison must have intended for himself and his partner.

". . . still up there a ways," Jerrison hissed. "Just keep looking."

Clint swore he heard another voice, but wasn't able to make out any words. If Jerrison was scheming with anyone, though, it meant his partner was nearby. And since both outlaws were in one place, that made Clint's job a little easier.

Rushing behind another few buildings, Clint raced through a tobacco shop and emerged on Franklin Avenue a little ways past Franklin Fixtures.

THIRTY-EIGHT

"Ain't nobody comin', Adams, and you know it!" Chris hollered.

In the store behind him, the outlaw could hear pipes hitting the floor and glass cases being shattered. After taking a few steps toward Sales Street, Chris fired off the last of his rounds and turned to rush into Franklin Fixtures.

"I think he skinned out of here," Chris said triumphantly. "Maybe he's scared."

"Or maybe he's getting reinforcements," Samuel said from behind one of the cases.

Reloading his .45, Jerrison grinned and took another look outside. "What reinforcements? The law's on our side, remember?"

Samuel grunted under his breath and pulled up a section of the floor. "All that means is we can't trust Flynt any more than this town can trust him. The fat prick is probably gonna string us up the first chance he gets."

"String you up, maybe," Chris replied with a smirk. "You're the one they think is a murderer."

When Samuel looked up at him, it was with enough

intensity in his eyes to melt Chris's head like a candle. "I wonder how they got that idea?"

"How the hell do I know?"

"It couldn't be you told someone that to keep the fire burning under my feet instead of yours."

Chris chuckled and took another look out the window. "In case you ain't noticed, both of us have been drawing the same amount of fire. And since Harvey couldn't get his pants on fast enough, that leaves only us two to try and dodge the bullets."

Samuel let out a measured breath and stuck both hands through the hole in the floorboards he'd pulled up.

"What've you found there?" Chris asked as he walked over to look across the broken counter.

"Strongbox," Samuel replied.

"Them plans inside?"

Lifting a dented metal box that wasn't big enough to hold a pair of men's shoes, Samuel said, "Not likely."

"Well, open it up anyways."

"We can take it with us. Adams is probably still coming after us."

Chris laughed and waved at the front window. "That whole street's clear. Adams is probably out trying to scrape up some more of these chickenshit locals to—"

The remainder of what Jerrison meant to say was swallowed up by the sound of wood being splintered and hinges being knocked from their screws. The back door of the shop was kicked in and Clint dove behind a display case as soon as he was through the splintered frame.

"Take the strongbox and get the hell outta here!" Chris shouted as he pointed his .45 at the spot where Clint had landed and fired a shot.

Samuel had his gun in hand when he got to his feet and

the strongbox was tucked under his arm. Starting to protest, he was cut short by a head shake from his partner.

"Just go!" Chris roared. After that, he pulled his trigger enough times to shatter every piece of glass in the display case.

Hopping over the broken counter, Samuel reached out and slapped his gun into Chris's free hand. "Meet back at the horses," Samuel said.

"Just clear a path for me. I won't be far behind." With that, Chris took hold of the gun Samuel had given him and started firing it as soon as his own pistol ran dry.

The little shop filled with the thunder from the pistols.

Sparks flew from the display case, because the fixtures in it were made of iron or brass.

Baring his teeth in a wide grin, Jerrison moved forward until he was close enough to look over the top of the case. He stood in his spot, waiting for Clint to make a move. After a few seconds, Jerrison stooped down to pick up a stray chunk of wood and he tossed it toward one end of the display case.

Nothing happened.

Keeping his head low, Jerrison rushed toward the other end of the display case with his gun up and ready to fire.

The only things on the floor behind all the broken brass and iron fixtures were more broken fixtures.

When he heard the rustling behind another display case, however, it was too late for Chris to do much of anything about it.

THIRTY-NINE

Clint stood up with his gun held at hip level, so it was just high enough to clear the top of the display case he'd been hiding behind. Thanks to the intimate knowledge he'd gained of the shop's floor plan, Clint had been able to crawl from one case to another without double-checking if he could stay out of sight. He'd made the switch while Chris was busy and now it was paying off.

"Don't take another step," Clint said. "It's all over."

Jerrison held his hands up, but didn't raise them any higher than shoulder level. He also didn't let go of his .45. "It ain't over 'til it's over. You should know that."

"It should have been over when I got the drop on you after you tried stealing my horse," Clint pointed out. "I was feeling generous that day and look where it got me."

"I'll tell you where it got you. It got you a chance to make out like a bandit."

"How do you figure?"

Latching on to the few extra seconds he'd bought for himself, Jerrison leaned forward and started to take a step toward Clint but stopped short when he saw the warning glare in Clint's eye. "We're gonna make a fortune selling some plans to a few very interested parties."

"What plans?"

"Plans for a bunch of safes being put together right here in Red Water. Them plans can be used to take apart them safes, just like they can be used to put them together."

"You're supposed to know how to do that?" Clint asked skeptically.

Without blinking an eye, Jerrison replied, "Hell, no, but the men we're selling the plans to know plenty and they're willing to pay. We got it all lined up."

"You mean Flynt's got it all lined up."

"Flynt barely lined up his own men to march them outta town," Jerrison scoffed. "That prick gets his percentage for it and that's it."

Sadly enough, Clint believed every word of that. He would have been more suspicious if the town's marshal was given any more credit than he was worth. "So you're trying to cut me in?" Clint asked.

Jerrison shrugged and glanced toward the front door. "You got the drop on me fair and square. It's either that or put a bullet in you."

"Or," Clint added, "you can tell a judge what you told me and then try bargaining your way out of jail."

Jerrison's lazy grin remained in place and he slowly shook his head. "I ain't the sort to fool about in a court-house," he said as he sneaked another glimpse at the door.

Clint didn't bother looking at the door. He could see enough from the corner of his eye to spot any motion coming from that direction and there wasn't anything happening on that side of the shop anyhow. "If you're waiting for your friend to come back for you," he said, "I think you're going to be disappointed. He would have rescued you by now if he could. Or if he still had his gun."

Finally, the smirk on Jerrison's face faded away. He gritted his teeth and clenched his fist around the gun in his hand.

"You've got a few rounds left, but I wouldn't advise you to try to burn them," Clint warned. "If you go to jail, at least you've got a chance. I truly don't believe all that murder talk Flynt was spouting. Any real posse would have caught the three of you a long time ago."

It hadn't been Clint's intention to goad Jerrison, but he simply couldn't help himself. Also, he didn't want to wait around forever because Samuel would find his way back to the shop eventually. Judging by the twitching muscles in Jerrison's face and arms, the situation would be resolved long before his partner decided to come back.

"I could'a killed you back at that camp," Jerrison snarled.

"You did your best and fell short. Don't make the same mistake twice."

Clint's last words hit a nerve and Jerrison didn't try to hide it. Each breath the outlaw took was more ragged than the last until he'd stoked his fire high enough to make a move.

Jerrison dropped to one knee and straightened his gun arm so he could sight along the top of his barrel.

Clint pulled his trigger out of reflex, but that shot hissed through the air where Jerrison would have been if he'd remained standing. Fortunately for him, Jerrison's shot was also thrown off when he'd dropped down and it sparked against one of the pipes on display in the case Clint was standing behind.

Taking a fraction of a second to shift his aim, Clint fired once more and put a round through the upper portion of Jerrison's chest. The impact knocked the outlaw straight back, causing him to hit the floor with a loud thump. Jerrison's finger clenched around his trigger again to fire a shot into the ceiling.

Moving around the display case, Clint checked the front door and found nothing but a few curious locals trying to get a look inside from the street. He stepped over to Jerrison and took the gun from the outlaw's hand.

Seeing the placement of Jerrison's chest wound, Clint crouched to the man's level and quickly asked, "Where's your partner?"

"That . . . son of a bitch . . ." Jerrison croaked while coughing up some pink, foamy blood. "He left me . . . here. He actually . . . left me." Before Clint needed to ask again, the outlaw snapped, "There's a lot across Sales Street that's . . . down some other avenue. I don't know which avenue but . . . our horses are there. That's where I'm supposed to . . ."

When Jerrison's voice trailed off and his eyes clouded over, Clint knew the outlaw was dead. Rather than waste any time mourning the loss of someone who would have gladly traded places with him, Clint rushed out of the shop and reloaded his Colt on his way across Sales Street.

FORTY

Samuel wasn't quite the traitor that Jerrison had assumed he was. When Clint hurried down the avenue directly across from Franklin, he found the last remaining outlaw leading two horses back toward Sales Street. Upon spotting Clint, Samuel stopped and calmly met Clint's gaze.

"You killed him, didn't you?" Samuel asked.

Clint kept his eyes level and his shoulders squared when he replied, "He didn't leave me much choice."

"Now you're here to kill me."

"I'll give you the same chance I gave your other partners," Clint told him. "You can speak up for what you've done and do your part to make sure Flynt doesn't wear a badge again. There'll probably be some jail time, but that's the price you pay."

"Or?"

"Or you can try to get away from me," Clint said plainly. "Maybe you'll do better than your partners. Maybe you won't."

Samuel's eyes darted to Clint's gun and then jumped right back up again. "You've got the pistol and Chris has mine. That is, he had it."

Clint could see the fire was still burning inside the man. It would keep burning even if Clint managed to get Samuel tied up alongside Laramie and would only grow brighter until Samuel found a way to get loose and get the drop on Clint. A fire like that kept men going and Clint knew better than to try to stamp it out. Since he also didn't like the idea of shooting Samuel just to make things easier, there was only one alternative.

Clint needed to convince Samuel that his fire burned just a little hotter.

Nodding slowly, Clint opened the cylinder of his Colt and dropped five of his six bullets to the ground. Each one hit the dirt until only one remained in the chamber. "This one is just for insurance," Clint said as he closed the cylinder. Once he'd done that, Clint held his gun arm out to one side, opened his hand, and let the Colt hit the ground amid all the fallen bullets.

Samuel looked down at the gun and then up at Clint. His brow furrowed as he tried to make sense of what he was seeing. "You want me to believe you'll just let me leave?"

"I'm not stepping aside and letting you do anything. If you want to come along with me and face up to your crimes like a man, you can do that. If you want to take a run at me, then do it now instead of waiting for a chance to hit me when my back's turned."

When he said those words, Clint could feel them grating against Samuel the way other words had grated against both of his partners. While Samuel didn't react as harshly as the other two outlaws, he fixed his eyes on Clint and stalked forward. He let go of the horses' reins and dropped his hands to just above waist level.

Clint knew what was coming.

Samuel wasn't as stupid as Laramie or as brash as Jerrison, but he wasn't about to hand himself over and quietly

be marched off to face a jury. Considering everything that
had been tacked onto the three outlaws, it didn't matter anymore which crimes the men had committed or not. They'd
gone far enough to make sure their chances were slim to
none.

Samuel came at Clint like a flicker of lightning. He
crouched down low and put all of his weight behind one
shoulder at the last possible second as Clint tried to twist
out of his way. Adjusting to Clint's movement, Samuel extended an arm and slammed it against Clint's stomach like
a club.

The impact was fast and powerful enough to rob Clint of
his next breath. By the time Clint hopped away and turned
to face Samuel again, the man was taking another swing at
him.

Before Clint could react, he felt Samuel's fist pound
against the same spot that had just been hit. One blow piled
on top of another sent a wave of dull pain through Clint's
entire body and also made his legs unsteady beneath him.

Samuel sensed what he'd done and moved in closer to
capitalize on it. One fist snapped out for Clint's jaw, but
Clint was able to turn his head before catching the punch
on the chin. Samuel's other fist snapped out, setting up a
flurry of jabs against Clint's chest like he was tenderizing a
slab of beef.

For a few seconds, Clint could only weather the blows
while trying to stay on his feet. When he felt what could
have been a rib cracking, Clint wondered if he hadn't made
a mistake in giving Samuel a fighting chance. Then again,
if he hadn't had this fight now, it would have occurred at
another time before they parted ways.

Before Clint's mind could wander too far, he sucked in a
breath and shook himself out of the fog closing in on him
from all sides. Turning his upper body while dropping his

left arm, Clint was able to snag one of Samuel's arms as he delivered another punch. Once Samuel's violent rhythm had been broken, he slammed a boot down toward Clint's foot.

Clint was just able to swing that leg back so Samuel's heel stomped against the ground. He cinched his arm even tighter around Samuel's wrist and then delivered a straight punch to the man's jaw. As soon as Samuel recoiled from that impact, Clint swept his foot against the back of Samuel's legs to take them out from under him. Rather than let go of Samuel's arm, Clint lowered himself with him and pulled back his free hand in preparation for what had to be the finishing punch.

A glint of steel caught Clint's eye and he pulled away from Samuel just as the outlaw swung a knife at his stomach. If Clint hadn't let go of the man's arm and moved, he would have been gutted on the spot. As it was, he only felt the blade rake across his midsection and heard it shred through his shirt.

Clint backed away some more while touching the spot where he'd been cut. He didn't want to take his eyes off Samuel, so he just glanced at his fingers. There was enough blood there to let him know he'd been cut, but not enough to worry about.

Samuel didn't let Clint get his bearings before rushing at him with the blade held in a low grip. He slashed out with the knife once and caught nothing but air. While Clint was still reeling backward, Samuel threw a quick feint and then lunged with the intention of driving the blade up under Clint's ribs.

Taking one more step back and then planting a foot, Clint snapped both arms down to catch the hand wielding the blade being swung at him. Samuel was strong, but Clint was able to stop the outlaw's hand before it buried the knife into his belly.

For a moment, Clint thought he could end the fight. He had a good grip on Samuel's wrist, but the outlaw simply flipped the knife to his other hand and raised the blade over his head in preparation for a downward stab. Clint let go of Samuel's wrist as if it were a snake getting ready to bite him. He was then barely able to cross both arms and raise them in time to block the incoming stab. Samuel's arm bounced off Clint's and then the outlaw immediately took a step back to give himself some room.

As Clint watched, Samuel shifted his grip on the blade half a dozen times. One moment, he was holding the blade straight out to take a few quick lunges. The next, he'd switched so the blade ran up along his forearm and he could swing it in an arc aimed for Clint's eyes or chest. Every so often, Clint would take a swing at Samuel, but for every time his knuckles landed, there was another time his blow was deflected and he got another cut for his efforts.

Blood seeped into Clint's sleeves and several other sections of his shirt, but the wounds were all shallow. The way the fight was going, however, he wasn't going to bet on his luck to hold up forever. Setting his jaw in a firm line, Clint threw a few more high punches at Samuel's head. After Samuel shifted both arms up to that level, Clint snuck in a straight kick to the outlaw's stomach.

Clint's boot landed solidly, driving a good portion of the air from Samuel's lungs while also forcing him back several paces until his back hit a wall.

Bouncing off the wall like a ricochet, Samuel flipped the knife around to grab it by the blade and then cocked it back next to his ear.

Knowing what was coming next, Clint bent down to scoop up his Colt. He got the weapon in his hand, looked up, and aimed it as if he were pointing his finger. By that time, Samuel had thrown the knife at him.

Clint squeezed his trigger and felt the Colt buck against his palm.

The round hit the blade with a loud clang to send a quick flash of sparks into the air.

Samuel's knife flew to the side, leaving Clint with a smoking gun in his hand. Before Samuel could make another move, Clint plucked a fresh round from his gun belt and slipped it into the cylinder.

Raising his hands and closing his eyes as if he didn't expect to open them again, Samuel let out a breath and waited for the end.

FORTY-ONE

Clint knocked at the door to the root cellar, waited a few seconds, and then knocked again. Even after all of that, he was still greeted by the barrel of a gun when he opened the door. Sticking his neck out, he waited for his eyes to adjust to the shadows and said, "It's only me, Baker."

Baker huddled in the cellar with his back to Laramie and both hands wrapped around his gun. It took him a bit longer to adjust to the change in light and even when he did, he still seemed nervous. "Who's that behind you?" Baker asked. "Do you need any help?"

"Yeah," Clint replied. "I need you to find me another chair."

With that, Clint stepped inside and away from the door so he could let Samuel walk past him. Clint held his Colt in an easy grip that kept the pistol ready but not directly aimed at his prisoner.

Samuel's head drooped forward and he stooped down to keep from bumping it against the top of the cellar. His hands were tied behind his back, but there was enough slack in the ropes to let him move well enough on his own. Once inside the cellar, Samuel stopped and locked eyes with Baker.

Seeing the puzzled expression on Baker's face, Clint explained, "We had ourselves a tussle, but came to an understanding."

"A tussle?" Baker scoffed. "Looks like you two kicked the hell out of each other."

"That's another way to put it," Clint said with a shrug. "Have you had any problems?"

"Some of the girls have been coming down here to check on us," Baker replied. "They did a good job of keeping my friend here in line."

"That bitch slapped me for no good reason," Laramie whined from the back of the cellar.

Baker turned to look over his shoulder and said, "You asked her to suck your . . ." Turning back to Clint, he said, "He didn't stay quiet when he should have, so he got a shot in the mouth."

Clint couldn't help but smirk at that. "A common downfall among many young men."

"Especially that one," Samuel grumbled. "Things would'a been a lot easier if he could keep his trap shut."

"Aw, go to hell. You could'a stayed on your damn plantation or wherever the hell you was before me an' Chris let you trail along behind us."

The more Laramie talked, the heavier the air within the cellar became. When the kid stopped to take a breath, Clint swore he could see steam coming from Samuel's collar.

"Why don't you shut the hell up before you get a gag or a fist shoved down your throat," Clint said. "Or I could just untie Samuel's hands and lock the two of you in here. He's been agreeable enough for me to trust him that much."

Laramie's face paled and his eyes widened.

Although Clint couldn't get a straight view of Samuel's face, he could guess well enough how he looked when he heard the menacing tone in the man's voice.

"I'd like that." Samuel growled.

Baker looked back and forth between the two prisoners. "I . . . uhh . . . I don't think that's a good idea."

"All right, then," Clint replied. "Think you could scrounge up another chair and some more rope?"

"Yes. I think I could do that." As Baker walked past Samuel, he kept his gun at the ready. He backed out of the cellar until he was too far to see anyone inside. After that, he ran toward Joan's Emporium.

Clint nudged Samuel's shoulder to get him moving. As the black man got closer to Laramie, the kid squirmed in his chair.

"If you're gonna let him take a swing at me, at least let me defend myself!" Laramie whined.

"I don't know if I can hold him back," Clint warned, even though Samuel had yet to make a truly threatening move.

Samuel must have been glaring at the kid awfully hard, because Laramie had yet to stop squirming within the layers of ropes that bound him.

"I could make sure you stay in one piece if you tell me the rest of Marshal Flynt's plan," Clint said.

Gritting his teeth, Laramie forced himself to sit still. It seemed to help when he looked at Clint instead of Samuel. "I won't be known as some yellow son of a bitch who gives up his partners. You may have caught that one, but Chris is still out there. Just wait until he finds you! He'll shoot you so full of holes you won't—"

"Your other partner is dead," Clint said.

Those words hit Laramie like a bucket of cold water. His face was frozen in the defiant expression he'd worn when tossing his last few threats at Clint, but the spark was quickly fading from his eyes. Finally, the kid asked, "Really?"

Samuel nodded once when Laramie looked at him.

"If'n you killed Chris, then you'll just kill us," Laramie said. "I ain't gonna say a damn thing."

"If I wanted to kill you two, I would have done it already," Clint pointed out. "Flynt's a crooked lawman and they tend to draw a lot more fire during a trial."

"Flynt's coming back tomorrow," Samuel said.

"You piece of shit!" Laramie spat.

Clint walked over to shove his bandanna into the kid's mouth. Once that was done, he turned to look at Samuel. "Go on."

"I'll tell you the rest, but only if I stand trial for what I done," Samuel said. "I ain't gonna answer for what other folks say I done."

"You're a horse thief," Clint pointed out. "You also robbed that store and tried to steal those safe plans. Whatever Flynt had in mind for that safe maker, I'll have to assume you were in on it, too."

Samuel nodded once. "You'd be right with all of that."

"All right, then," Clint replied. "When I turn you over to a real lawman, that's what you'll go in for. I can't guarantee anything during your trial, though."

"I got to answer for what I've done. I knew it might come to that, but I won't stay put to hang for some trumped-up bullshit anyone like Flynt tries to put on me."

"Fair enough. Start talking."

FORTY-TWO

After Baker arrived with a chair and rope for Samuel, he and Clint took turns watching the prisoners. Having Samuel next to Laramie was even better than stuffing a bandanna in his mouth. The kid seemed too nervous to say much of anything now that his partner was close enough to kick him. The fact that Chris wasn't on his way made Laramie pull his head into his shell even further.

When he wasn't sitting in the doorway to the cellar, Clint climbed to the top of Joan's Emporium. There was a single room in the attic where Gertrude slept. It was a neat little space with a small bed and a large window that had a perfect view of Red Water. She allowed Clint and Baker to sit up there in shifts to watch for any sign of the posse returning to town.

According to Samuel, Flynt was supposed to keep all the men away from Red Water until the next afternoon. So far, Clint hadn't seen anything to make him believe Samuel was lying. He had no reason to believe Samuel would pass up a chance to escape, either, but there was certainly no love lost between Flynt and any of the three outlaws. On the few occasions the marshal's name had come up, Laramie and Samuel practically spat it out as if it left a bad taste in their mouths. When they spoke about the deputies, they might as well have been talking about slobbering dogs.

Clint was sitting in a rocker next to the attic window when Pearl walked into the room. The tall blonde was smiling when she approached Clint with a cup and pitcher in her hands.

"You look ready to start knitting something," Pearl said.

Clint looked down to find a half-finished sweater draped over one arm of his chair. "And it looks like I do pretty good work," he replied.

Approaching him, she said, "I brought you some water. There's some food downstairs, too, if you want it. Just some sandwiches, but they're pretty good."

"No thanks, but I'll take the water."

Accepting the cup from Pearl, Clint sipped the water and then shifted his eyes back to the window.

"Do you think those lawmen will be coming back?" she asked.

"They're not due until tomorrow, but I don't want to take any chances."

"Since Flynt will be expecting all hell to have broken loose around here, he'll probably be a little upset when he just finds one body." Noticing the questioning look in Clint's eyes, she added, "Baker and those other two did some talking when I brought them their sandwiches. Well, mostly the younger one."

"I'm surprised you didn't hear a lot more from that one when you had him all to yourself."

Pearl rolled her eyes and shook her head. "He could barely put two words together before tripping over his tongue. Once he did get going, he just did the same sort of bragging every other boy his age does."

"Once he got going, huh?"

There was no mistaking where Clint was headed with that. Pearl responded with a short laugh along with a bit of a blush in her cheeks. "As far as that goes . . . I think it may have been his first time."

"I'm sure he'd deny that with every breath in his body." Clint chuckled.

"He can deny it all he wants, but he . . . well . . . he struck me as a boy with high hopes and no experience. I get a lot of those."

Clint took another sip of water and said, "You do seem like a soft, pretty lady who won't bite."

"I will if the occasion calls for it," Pearl replied with a promising smile.

"I'm sure you're worth every penny, but . . ."

Reading Clint perfectly, Pearl took the cup from his hand and said, "You strike me as the sort of man that doesn't need to count pennies to get on a woman's good side. I haven't been with a man like that in a while."

As Pearl moved around to stand in front of him, Clint reached out to place his hand upon her hip. "And you do," he told her as he rubbed the curve of her buttocks, "have one hell of a good side."

She reached down to take hold of his wrists and guide his hands to her pert breasts. "Try this side. It's not so bad either."

Clint massaged her breasts and soon he felt her tugging at his belt. In no time at all, she had his pants down just enough to free his erection. Pearl lifted her skirts and eased down to let him slide into her. She let out a slow sigh and slipped her legs around so she could sit on his lap facing him.

The rocker moved slowly back and forth, allowing Clint to slip in and out of her. He took his time and held her in place with both hands. Pearl wrapped her legs around him and rested her head upon his shoulder. She shifted every now and then, but seemed perfectly content to just feel his hardness slowly moving in her.

"You think you can keep this up for a while?" she asked.

"I can sure try," Clint told her.

"Then, as a reward, I can tell you the rest of what I heard from those men in the root cellar."

Clint stopped moving and looked her in the eyes. "What did they say?"

Pearl smiled as if she'd just awakened from a deep sleep. "Not yet."

"If you heard something, I want to know about it. Otherwise, don't try to put one over on me."

"I'm not trying to pull anything," she assured him. Shifting her hips, Pearl managed to send a jolt through Clint without moving more than a few well-trained muscles. "Don't worry," she whispered. "We have all night and some of the morning."

Clint grabbed her in both hands, pumped halfway into her, and stopped. Just as she opened her eyes all the way, he thrust the rest of the way into her and stopped. "Tell me now, or you won't get any more."

She smiled and rubbed his shoulder. "I knew negotiating with you would be a hoot. Why don't we both go at the same time? I talk and you keep doing what you were doing."

Clint thrust into her a few more times, simply because he couldn't help himself. Pearl was true to her word and placed her lips against his ear to whisper her report between deep, grateful breaths.

FORTY-THREE

It was late in the morning when the four horses ambled toward the field about a quarter of a mile outside Red Water. The horses were in the deliberate, plodding rhythm of their casual gait and the riders on their backs were happy to let them keep ambling at their own pace.

The air was cool and damp, making it seem earlier than it truly was. There was easy laughter drifting among the riders and when the man at the front of the group motioned for them to stop, it was with a cordial wave.

"This is the spot, boys," Marshal Flynt said. "Matter of fact, I even see the marker."

Frank was the only other man wearing a badge, and he rode directly beside the marshal. Lefty and Arvin brought up the rear. The two posse members slouched in their saddles, doing nothing to hide the fact that they'd washed down their morning bacon with a few gulps of whiskey.

"Where's Tom?" Arvin asked. "You said he was supposed to meet up with us."

Bringing his horse to a stop next to a single post sticking from the ground at an angle, Flynt replied, "I ain't worried about that one. Adams and Baker were probably giving him too much trouble. Tom's either running them all the way out to Springston or burying them somewhere along the way."

"Whichever it is," Frank added, "them two won't be bothering us."

The two posse members shrugged. "More reward money for us," Arvin grunted. "Baker always was a busybody."

Flynt climbed down from his saddle as if he'd fallen from it. The irregular lumps of his stomach and torso made it seem easier for him to roll off his horse's strained back. "Well, now we know where that busybody stands. And now that I see where you men stand, I can find more work for ya. After today, there's gonna be plenty of work for all of us."

"If it's as easy as this posse," Lefty said, "you can count me in."

Flynt's liver lips curled into a smile as he huffed and waddled his way over to the post. Once there, he let out another series of grunts as he went through the arduous labor of squatting down to paw at the ground like a dog digging for a bone. Before long, his grunts became louder and then finally turned into a confused rumble.

"What's the matter?" Frank asked.

"They ain't here," Flynt said as if he was muttering to himself. After digging a few more hasty scoops from the ground, he hollered, "They ain't here!"

"What ain't there?" Arvin asked.

"The . . . what I was looking for," Flynt said.

Frank practically jumped down from his horse to rush over to the marshal's side. "They ain't there? Where the hell are they?"

"If I knew where they were, I'd have them in my damn hands, now wouldn't I?" Flynt snarled. "Stop asking stupid questions and start digging. They got to be nearby. Maybe the marker's just a bit off."

"Off from where?" Arvin asked.

Sighing impatiently, Lefty grunted, "This don't have to do with the reward money, does it?"

"There isn't going to be any reward money."

That voice had rolled in from somewhere else in the field like a stray breeze. It affected the posse more like a whirlwind, since it caused them all to spin around to search for its source. The men's eyes couldn't fix upon a specific target, but their faces were all pointed in roughly the same direction.

Flynt pulled in a wheezing breath, but wasn't able to let it out before the whirlwind rolled in again.

"The plans aren't there, Flynt, so you can stop looking."

"Adams?" Flynt shouted. "Is that you?"

The air was still enough for every little sound to be heard, and everyone in the group immediately heard the rustling coming from nearby.

"Yeah," Clint called from his new position. "It's me. Sounds like you thought I'd be dead."

Flynt smirked uncomfortably on the off chance that he could be seen. "Tom's got a hot head sometimes, that's all. You two never did seem to get along."

"Imagine that."

"Say . . . where is Tom?"

In the few seconds of silence that followed, Flynt motioned for his deputy to circle around toward the sound of Clint's voice. He motioned for the posse members to circle in another direction, but had to wave frantically at them until they started paying attention to him.

"Tom's in a different field," Clint replied.

"That'll cost you, Adams!" Flynt cried. "He was a lawman!"

"And what about those outlaws you all are supposed to be hunting?" Clint asked from a slightly different spot in the field. "Did you deputize them to keep their looting nice and legal?"

"What's that supposed to mean?" Lefty asked.

Turning to the posse member, Flynt snarled, "It don't mean shit. Adams killed Tom and now he's after the reward money."

"What were you looking for, Marshal?" Clint asked. "Buried treasure?"

"Yeah," Lefty said. "What were you looking for?"

Flynt swung his hand at Lefty and Arvin with enough force to create a breeze. "You men want to ask questions? Go do it on your own time! If you won't follow orders, then get the hell outta my sight!"

"You looking for someone who follows your orders?" Clint asked. "Try that wagon behind you."

Both Flynt and Frank spun around with their guns drawn. They didn't find Clint standing there, but they did see a small wagon parked about ten yards away. They approached the wagon, which was just big enough to hold a small load of barrels or a few piles of burlap sacks. Instead of any of those things, however, the cart now contained the crumpled body of Chris Jerrison.

As soon as Flynt saw whose corpse was in the wagon, he gritted his teeth and hissed, "Find Adams and gun him down. I'll pay extra to the man that drops that son of a bitch."

FORTY-FOUR

"Fan out!" Flynt bellowed. "This murderer killed Tom and now he's killed this man!"

"Who is that?"

"Will you shut your goddamn mouth, Lefty? Just do what I say! I'm the law around here and you do what I tell you!"

"Did you tell them about the deal you struck to sell those plans?" Clint asked.

This time, the voice was coming from a spot that was definitely closer and definitely to Flynt's left. The marshal jabbed his finger in that direction and traded his pistol for the shotgun hanging from his saddle.

"You're a liar and a murderer, Adams!" the marshal shouted. "You're just trying to get us to drop our guard."

"Why would I do that," Clint asked as he stood up just enough for his hat to rise above a patch of weeds, "when I could have killed you all by now?"

The entire posse fired at once. Lawmen and locals alike pulled their triggers until the air was filled with enough smoke to choke their horses. When they eased up a bit, Frank moved toward the spot where Clint had been. He made it less than three steps before Clint stood up and fired a single shot from his Colt.

Sparks flew from the gun in the deputy's hand as Clint's bullet knocked the pistol from his grasp. Without batting an eye, Clint put his second round through the meaty part of Marshal Flynt's shoulder. Although the lawman didn't drop his shotgun, he wasn't able to lift it either.

"This posse is a joke," Clint declared. "All you wanted to do was clear out the town so those outlaws could do some dirty work for you."

"What the hell are you talking about?" Flynt hollered. "You're the one firing on us!"

"Since you're the one who sent Tom to take me and Baker out of the way or bury us, I'm sure you can understand why I'm a little upset."

"That's preposterous!"

"No it ain't, Marshal," Lefty said. "You told us so yourself."

"And you went along for your cut of the reward," Flynt shot back.

"Now I'm thinkin' you weren't straight with us. And if you weren't straight with us about what you had planned, how do we know you wouldn't double-cross us?" Lefty asked.

Clint smiled and nodded. "A little slow, but he got there all the same. Looks like your posse is catching on."

"You're outgunned, Adams," Frank pointed out.

"Outnumbered, maybe," Clint admitted. "But I'd only be worried if you men didn't waste half your ammunition shooting at a hat on a stick."

That got the men nervous. The uneasiness worked through the entire posse like a slowly moving ripple crossing the top of a pond. Arvin and Lefty lowered their guns. Frank swallowed hard as he stared at his own gun lying on the ground. Flynt broke out in a cold sweat.

"Did the marshal tell you men that Laramie and his partners were in Red Water trying to steal plans for some safes that were bound for half a dozen banks in Kansas?" Clint asked.

"No," Arvin replied. "He didn't."

"Did he tell you those plans were supposed to be left here so he could pick them up?"

Lefty sat bolt upright and glared at the lawman. "He sure didn't. I knew you was after something in this damn field!"

"Adams can't prove anything!" Flynt whined. "He's after the reward."

"Anything you would have paid these men would have been a fraction of what you got for selling off those plans," Clint said. "And you weren't even planning on paying that if you could help it. I hear you intended on paying extra to Laramie or any of those outlaws if they killed off your posse after you got what you were after."

Suddenly, Lefty and Arvin started to squirm. They leaned forward in their saddles to get a look at the cart. Even though the cart was a little ways from them, it was small enough for them to be certain there was only one body in it.

"Where's the rest of them outlaws?" Arvin asked. "Weren't there supposed to be three of them?"

Clint grinned and locked eyes with the marshal. "That's right. There were three of them. I suppose the other two must still be about."

Flynt's eyes grew to the size of silver dollars. "Whatever they told you, it was a lie."

"Really? Then they just happened to go after Sven because they thought he was the richest man in town?"

"You mean that German blacksmith?" Lefty asked.

"Go on and tell your men the truth," Clint said. "That way they'll know why those other two outlaws are gunning for them."

"You mean Laramie and that black fella are still alive?" Frank asked.

Clint nodded. "And they were pretty mad the last time I saw them."

"Why'd you let them go?" Flynt whined.

"I figured I wasn't a member of the posse once Tom tried to get rid of me and Baker. Laramie got real talkative when he realized your plan wasn't going anywhere. Once that one in the cart was done in, the other two didn't care about safe plans anymore. They just wanted blood. Still do, I suppose."

Flynt's breathing was so labored that it was louder than the wind. "All right, Adams. You win. We were out to sell those plans, but I'll cut you in on the profit. I'll cut you all in! Let's just find those other two before they kill us."

"They just want you, Flynt. Well," Clint added, "you and anyone else wearing a badge around here."

Flynt and his deputy Frank couldn't tear their badges off quick enough. They threw them to the ground along with their guns. "We can all walk away from this," Flynt pleaded. "There's no reason we can't just forget this ever happened."

Shrugging, Clint said, "I'm leaving town anyway. You're the ones that need to worry about those outlaws finding you."

"Fine, then. We'll leave, too."

"But . . ." Frank protested.

Flynt silenced him with a wave. "We'll leave! Just square things up between us and you won't never see us again."

Clint narrowed his eyes. "How do I know you won't just try to kill me the next chance you get? Maybe we should just have it out right now."

Unable to think of anything to say, the marshal climbed into his saddle and moved his horse away. Frank followed him. Once there was some distance between them, they dug their heels into their horses' sides and were off like they'd been shot from a cannon. Now only Arvin and Lefty remained. The two locals looked at each other, the fleeing lawmen, and then at Clint.

"What the hell are we supposed to do now?" Lefty asked.

Clint picked up his hat and examined all the holes that had been shot through it. "First, you might want to go to the field that's about half a mile west of here. It's the one with the scarecrow. Tom's been tied to that thing for a while and must be getting awfully anxious by now. After that, you'll probably want to scrounge up some new lawmen."

Clint walked away from the two locals to the spot where Eclipse was waiting. Neither of the former posse members made a move to stop him. In fact, they seemed too confused to do much of anything but stare at the old cart and its gruesome contents.

It was a short ride to the bluff overlooking the field where Jerrison's body had been left. Baker stood atop the bluff with a rifle propped against him and a wide smile on his face. As soon as Clint was close enough, Baker ran forward and said, "They skinned out without a fight. That is, unless you count the shots they fired at your hat. I can't believe that was so easy!"

"I can," Clint replied. "Someone who went through so much trouble to distract anyone capable of holding a gun while hiring someone like Laramie to do the work obviously didn't want a fight."

"I suppose so." Nodding toward the horses behind him, Baker asked, "What should we do with them?"

Clint looked over there to find Baker's horse and another horse carrying both Laramie and Samuel. The two outlaws were bound and gagged, tied to each other, and draped sideways over the horse's back. "I intended on turning them in. They're still horse thieves, but they're probably not worth half as much as Flynt was saying."

"Then I might as well go along with you," Baker said with a shrug. "Half of a little reward is better than a lot of a made up one. Besides, the best place to turn these fellas in is Wichita. You could use some help in getting them there and I already told the missus I'd be gone for a while."

Letting out a heavy sigh, Clint said, "Wichita, huh? I wonder if I can put up with Laramie for that long . . ."

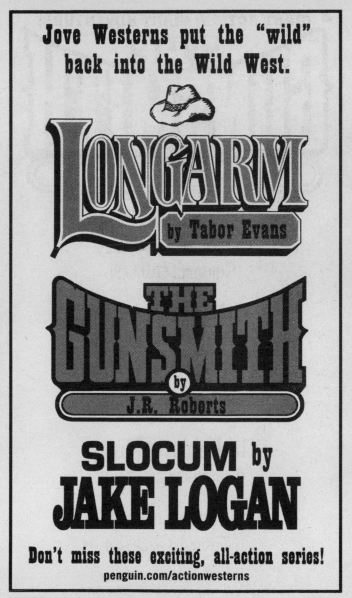

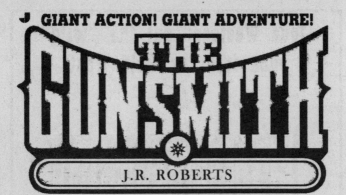

GIANT ACTION! GIANT ADVENTURE!

THE GUNSMITH

J.R. ROBERTS

Little Sureshot And
The Wild West Show
(Gunsmith Giant #9)

Dead Weight
(Gunsmith Giant #10)

Red Mountain
(Gunsmith Giant #11)

The Knights of Misery
(Gunsmith Giant #12)

The Marshal from Paris
(Gunsmith Giant #13)

penguin.com/actionwesterns